"**If your grandmother really is sick, and we can make her last days happy by pretending to get married, I'd say it's worth it.**"

"*Pretending* to get married? Are you suggesting we lie to her?"

Matt shrugged impatiently, the simple gesture making her feel she was being unreasonable. "Does it matter? If I have a choice between lying to her and making her miserable, I'll go with the lie. What harm could it do?"

Joanna stared at him, almost unable to believe he was really suggesting this. The idea was preposterous. It was out of the question.

She was still working on getting over Matt. Marrying him wouldn't help the healing process.

Hannah Bernard always knew what she wanted to be when she grew up—a psychologist. After spending an eternity in university studying toward that goal, she took one look at her hard-earned diploma and thought, "Nah. I'd rather be a writer." She has no kids to brag about, no pets to complain about and only one husband, who any day now will break down and agree to adopt a kitten.

Books by Hannah Bernard

HARLEQUIN ROMANCE®
3762—BABY CHASE
3774—THEIR ACCIDENTAL BABY
3792—MISSION: MARRIAGE

THE HONEYMOON PROPOSAL
Hannah Bernard

HARLEQUIN®

TORONTO • NEW YORK • LONDON
AMSTERDAM • PARIS • SYDNEY • HAMBURG
STOCKHOLM • ATHENS • TOKYO • MILAN • MADRID
PRAGUE • WARSAW • BUDAPEST • AUCKLAND

ISBN 0-373-03814-3

THE HONEYMOON PROPOSAL

First North American Publication 2004.

Copyright © 2004 by Hannah Bernard.

www.eHarlequin.com

Printed in U.S.A.

PROLOGUE

WAS it a law that the phone absolutely had to ring a few minutes after Grandma had closed her bedroom door to take a nap? Joanna lunged for the receiver, managing to snatch it up after only two rings had blared through the house. "Hello?"

"Hello, Jo."

Matt.

Joanna's hand clenched around the phone and she almost hung up. She'd somehow avoided him for three days—and now he'd managed to reach her at her grandmother's house.

But Grandma *was* his godmother after all, it was only natural for him to be calling here.

"Hello. One moment, I'll get Grandma."

"Wait! I'm calling to talk to you."

Dammit. She leaned back against the wall and closed her eyes, concentrating on keeping her voice level and calm. "I see. How did you know I was here?"

"I didn't, but it was worth a try. You're not answering your home phone, or your cell phone or your e-mail. I was running out of options."

Jo gritted her teeth. "If Grandma had caller ID we wouldn't be talking."

"Believe me, Jo. I know. I was the one your neighbors threatened to call the cops on yesterday, remember?"

Joanna grinned without pleasure and headed toward

the kitchen in order to get even further away from her grandmother's bedroom. Grandma didn't need to hear this, even if it would never escalate into a shouting match. Jo was too civilized for shouting matches. Nope, no screaming, just cool and calm conversation, icicles dripping off every word she said. "Your father called security on me at work, why shouldn't my neighbors call the cops on you?"

A tiny sound shimmered through the line, and her nervous brain translated it into a click. Her gaze flashed in the direction of her grandmother's bedroom. Could she have picked up the extension?

"Jo, you're not even giving me a chance," Matt continued, the same impatient irritation in his voice as before. He didn't get it, did he? He didn't have a clue about what this mess had done to her life. "Do you have any idea what I'm dealing with here? I have my hands full with the board, with the investigation, with finding out what really happened and how you got involved. It didn't help when you stormed out, and now you're saying we're over and refusing to talk to me—"

"Ssshhh!" she hissed, suspicion blooming and even diverting her attention from the barb of *how you got involved.* There *had* been a click on the line. She was sure of it. "Shut up. Wait."

"What?"

"Sssssh!"

Covering the speaker with her hand, Jo tiptoed upstairs to her grandmother's room and listened. There was no sound. She slowly turned the knob and pushed the door open. The drapes were pulled and the room was darkened, but she could make out the shape of Grandma in her bed, turned away from her with a blanket up to her neck. She stood still for a few moments, but the old lady didn't move. The phone was within her reach, so she might have picked up and put it back down again—was the cord swaying?

No. Or if it was, it had to be a draft from the window. Grandma wasn't the type to hide her interference, anyway. If she'd heard anything, she'd have come right out and demanded to know what was going on.

Jo pulled the door quietly shut, relieved that Grandma hadn't been listening in. She wasn't ready for Grandma to know she'd broken up with Matt. Grandma would ask questions. She'd probe and poke in wounds that hadn't healed yet, and she *would* meddle.

Grandma would have to be told, of course, but not right now. In a few days, when she was more composed over the whole thing, Jo would tell her. Now wasn't the right time.

"Jo?" Matt was saying when she raised the phone back to her ear. "What's wrong?"

She hurried back downstairs to the kitchen before speaking again. "Nothing."

"How are you doing, Jo?"

The question almost made her anger spill over, but with the self-restraint of a lifetime of practice she managed to contain it and keep her voice as calm and as chilly as a snowman's nose. "How am I doing? You mean, apart from the fact that you ruined my life?"

"Don't be so melodramatic," he said impatiently. "You're overreacting."

"I'm *overreacting?* I'm being *melodramatic?* I lost my job, had security invade my office and to top it all off, my…'' Her what? What had Matt been to her? ''My *lover*,'' she ended up saying with a sardonic twist in her voice, ''doesn't even believe in me. And you're surprised I want you out of my life?''

''I do believe in you…'' Matt broke off and swore. ''Why can't you trust me? Look—I'll come over tonight and we'll talk. Will you please let me in this time?''

He was trying to use charm on her. It wouldn't work. Not now, when she knew the truth about what he felt for her—when she knew he'd rather have her accused of a crime than admit they were a couple. But she wouldn't bring that up now—bruised pride wasn't the most comfortable emotion to have trampled on. ''We've had this conversation before, Matt. There's nothing to talk about. I'm not interested in having a fight.''

''You never are. Maybe that's the problem. We need to have a real fight.''

''We don't need anything. There is no we. If there ever was a we, we're over. Don't call me again. Bye.''

Matt cursed and his voice rose. ''No way. This is *not* over, Jo—''

She didn't hear another word, because the phone was firmly back in its cradle and her back was turned to it.

CHAPTER ONE

Five weeks later

SHE would have to see him again.

Joanna twined together curses in the most creative manner she could think of as she yanked the cordless phone off its stand and strode to the living room, to the security of the sofa, complete with an old scruffy blanket in case she needed additional comfort.

Seeing Matt again. The thought almost managed to nudge the burning worry about Grandma from her mind. Almost.

She sank into the sofa, and pulled her knees to her chest, clutching the phone in one hand. She reached for the ancient comforter lying across the back of the sofa and pulled it over her shoulders, huddling under it, suddenly feeling cold. A painful pounding in her temples had started as soon as her grandmother had made the request. She wasn't surprised. If ever there was an occasion to get a migraine headache, this was it.

She stared at the phone in her hand, amazed that her fingers weren't trembling. She would have to call Matt, and ask him to come over.

This was not a phone call she wanted to make. He was not a man she wanted to see again. Too much had happened, and after only five weeks the hurt and anger hadn't even begun to fade.

But she had no choice. Grandma did want to see

him. And he was her godson, her late husband's nephew, probably her favorite person in the world.

Of course she would call him. There was no question. For Grandma, she would, even if her own personal preference was to replace that two-minute phone call with a whole afternoon of root canals. Or a casual stroll across hot coals. Or two full hours of public speaking. Or...

She gritted her teeth, realizing she was procrastinating.

She'd do it now. Right this minute while shock was still running her emotions, or courage would leap out the window into the early-evening dusk and never return. This wasn't a big deal. It was absurd to find her heart racing in anticipation of hearing his voice again.

It was over. She was over him. "It's over," she muttered to herself, and it almost became the truth when she heard her own voice say the words. It was over.

She took a deep breath, and with eyes half-closed, made the call.

It was a melancholic—and annoying—discovery that she still knew his number by heart. Five long weeks had passed, but her fingers still punched the series of numbers as easily as they'd ever done. As easily as they'd done when this was the number she called just to hear his voice, when the warmth of him, the heat of his feelings for her, had seemed to reach her through the phone lines no matter what the distance was between them.

Now he was a stranger, the distance internal, emotional instead of geographical, but even more real. She needed to remember that, even as her mind recalled the way his voice used to alter the moment he heard hers, from the distracted, hurried voice of a busy businessman to the warm, loving one a man reserved for his woman.

She squeezed her eyes shut and pressed the phone hard against her ear. It was over, she repeated to herself. Now he was nothing to her, just her grandmother's godson, a friend of the family. That was all!

Still, she was just about to lose her nerve and end the call when he picked up the phone. The sound of his voice caused her heart to halt in her chest as truth grabbed her by the nose and forced her to face reality.

Over him? Hah!

Nope, she wasn't over him.

Not even close.

She'd almost managed to convince herself she was, but that was because she hadn't seen him, hadn't heard from him. Grandma had his picture on the mantelpiece, between her pictures of Grandpa and of Jo herself, but Jo had managed to tilt it ever so slightly, so his laughing green eyes didn't mock her every time she stepped into that room.

But now his voice was in her ear, and her entire system was going crazy.

His voice sounded the same. Brisk, slightly absent, hurried, impatient when he had to repeat the hello because she didn't respond right away, her voice having tightened and her breath hitched. She cursed herself for letting him affect her that way. It had only been a few weeks, she reminded herself. Time would fix this. Broken hearts did heal. Didn't they?

Maybe seeing him again now, seeing him as a stranger, not *hers,* would be the jolt she needed. Yes. Maybe.

It could happen, right?

"Matt... I... Matt..." she croaked, then bit her lip hard. That was not what she'd meant to say. She'd meant to be cool and distant and formal, call him Matthew instead of Matt, and inform him of the situation, detached and matter-of-fact.

She closed her eyes. Instead she'd whispered his name as a reverent mantra, just as she'd done when...

No. Those memories belonged in the compost section of her brain. She didn't want to remember. She didn't want to remember anything of their months together, especially not the warmth of his shoulder under her lips, the surprised smile he sent her when she kissed him unexpectedly, or those mornings at his apartment, the way he'd used the extra ten minutes the snooze button gave him to wrap his arms around her and hold on tightly, whispering into her ear that it would have to last him through the entire day with her all the way on the other side of the office.

Ouch. She yanked on the short hair at her temple to punish herself. That compost heap was active today.

Maybe she should just hang up, and hope he wouldn't know who was calling. She could get someone else to phone Matt. Grandma still had enough strength to lift a phone after all, she could probably make the call herself.

Matt's voice changed, grew louder, as if he'd gripped the phone and pressed it closer to his face. "Hello? Jo? Joanna? Is that you?"

Joanna grimaced as she mentally crossed hanging up anonymously off her list of options. He recognized her voice. She should have expected no less, but it was still a shock to hear her name on his lips, his tone surprised and incredulous.

Not angry, but slightly wary. It had been angry before. Not at first: then, there had been only surprise, annoyance and irritation, and a whole lot of brisk efficiency as he worked to smooth things over, to get her out of the way, to hush up the issue instead of coming to her rescue. The anger hadn't come until she'd told him it was over, that she couldn't keep seeing someone who didn't trust her, someone who wouldn't stand up and admit to their relationship even when it could clear her of a crime. *If you believed in me, you would stand by me,* she'd told him, the pain in her heart emerging as fury disguised in cold dismissal.

Of course, what she'd really meant was that if he'd *loved* her, he'd have stood by her, just as she'd kept silent about their involvement until he got back—for his sake. The CEO shouldn't be involved with one of his employees, and she wouldn't expose him without his agreement—even though it had cost her both her job and the friendships she'd forged there.

She hadn't minded at the time, in the certainty that he'd clear things up when he got back. If he'd trusted her—if he'd loved her, he would have.

The point was moot, of course—he'd done neither.

But this wasn't about them. This was about Grandma.

"Jo?" Matt repeated, his voice growing impatient. "It's you, isn't it?"

She clenched her hand around the phone and cleared her throat. "Yes. It's me. Hello, Matthew. I'm calling because… It's my grandmother. I'm at her house now, I've been staying a few days—well, almost two weeks. She hasn't been well lately. She wants to see you. She says she..." She paused to swallow the lump in her throat, but nevertheless the words were nothing more than a croak, betraying the tears gathering in her eyes. "Matt—she's probably just being overdramatic, you know what she's like sometimes, but...she says she needs to see you before she dies."

There was silence only for a second. "I'll be there ASAP," he said curtly, and hung up without a goodbye.

Left with a dial tone, Jo let her hand fall to her side and pried her fingers away from the phone. She took a deep breath, not knowing if she felt relief at having this over with or panic at knowing he was on his way. *Snap out of it*, she ordered herself and made her way toward the guest room where her grandmother was resting. Grandma had asked to see Matt. That was the only thing that mattered.

"Is he coming?" her grandmother asked, her blue eyes just as bright and alive now as they'd ever been. She was propped up on some pillows, looking tiny in the large canopy bed, a Walkman with an audio book lying on her lap, the headphones incongruous around her narrow neck. Crossword puzzle books were heaped on the nightstand. Grandma worked hard at keeping her mind active, and she succeeded.

Unfortunately, the body was no longer cooperating. Grandma, who always took pride in getting up early, looking her best at all times and keeping herself busy throughout the day, hadn't felt well enough to get dressed in more than a robe and slippers for a couple of weeks now. Jo had arrived for a visit almost two weeks ago, and hadn't left since, except to go to work.

"Yes, Grandma. He's on his way," Jo confirmed as she sat down in her usual spot at the foot of the bed. "He said he'd be here soon." She glanced at the clock on the wall. "Of course, he might not be here until tomorrow. He hung up so quickly, I didn't get a chance to ask him about his definition of ASAP." She grimaced. "Nothing new there."

Her grandmother smiled. "I know. He works too hard, Jo. You'll have to change that. A man doesn't always realize the importance of spending time with his woman. Not until it's too late. Hasn't it been a while since you saw him last yourself?"

"Matt's very busy," Jo evaded, forcing a smile to her face. "But he's on his way. You know he always makes time for his favorite old crone."

As expected, Grandma chortled at the old joke. "Well, I hate to bother him, but I need to see that boy." Her eyes narrowed on Joanna's face. "There are things we need to discuss. I need to talk to him about the way he intends to treat my granddaughter for the rest of his life. I have a few ground rules. Such as spending at least some of his weekends with his woman—something he hasn't been doing recently, has he? You didn't leave the house all weekend and he didn't come to see you at all."

Joanna looked down on the bedspread, trying to hide her expression. Her omission of truth was coming back to haunt her. She still hadn't figured out how to wriggle out of this one. "Grandma, Matt's been very busy recently. I accept that, just as he accepts it when I'm busy. That's life. He doesn't need ground rules. We're both quite happy with the way things are.''

''I'm not leaving this world without discussing you with him. You two are spending your lives together, and I have some hints and tips. I lived thirty-seven years with your grandfather, you know.'' She patted Joanna's hand. ''In fact, I have plenty of tips for you on how to tame bad-tempered men.''

''Matt isn't bad-tempered,'' Jo said, shocked to find a small smile pull at her lips. ''He's stubborn and always tends to think he's right, but he doesn't have a bad temper.''

''He has a strong control of his temper, but he also has strong emotions,'' Grandma muttered. ''A roaring lion when it comes to protecting his woman, just you wait and see.''

Protecting his woman. Jo's smile faltered. That was one thing Matt hadn't done, and the truth of it was a constant sting somewhere inside. Grandma was right—Matt would stop at nothing to protect his woman. It all went to show she'd never been *his*. Not in the way that really counted.

''The most important thing is always to make time for just the two of you,'' Grandma whispered, as if sharing the deepest confidence. ''Arrange baby-sitting, and make sure you have regular quality time together.''

''*Baby-sitting?*''

''I know I'm getting ahead of myself here, you probably want an engagement and a wedding before the babies—and I don't disagree, but I don't have much time to impart all my hard-earned wisdom, so there you are.''

''You have plenty of time,'' Joanna said firmly,

trying to keep her fear from showing. Her grandmother was convinced death was on the other side of each breath. The doctor just shrugged. At her age, anything was certainly possible, he'd said, but there was nothing immediately terminal in her condition. However, he had confided in Jo, in his experience, people often sensed these things.

And Grandma's conviction was contagious. Even now, she just smiled indulgently at Joanna's objection. "No, I don't, girlie. I don't mind, and I hope you don't plan on spending too much time grieving for me. I'm sure the other side is more fun. I'll hold a spot for you and Matt."

"We still need you on this side, Grandma. Don't even think about opening that door."

"I'm not. Not until I've talked to my Matt. Is the house clean?"

Joanna felt her frown crumble into a reluctant smile. Sometimes her grandmother's mind was very predictable. "Yes, Grandma. The house is clean. We have nothing to be embarrassed about."

"Good. We don't want Matt to think we're slobs, do we?"

"He won't."

Her grandmother sighed, and laid her head back against the pillow. "I'm so useless these days," she muttered. "I need a nap again. You'll bring Matt here the minute he arrives, Joanna, won't you?"

"Of course." Joanna kissed her grandmother's cheek and stood up. "You just ring the bell if you need anything."

Grandma muttered something, already half asleep. Jo made sure the bell was within reach and tiptoed out of the room.

She was tired. Her grandmother wasn't a lot of work. She could take care of her own basic needs, and only required Joanna to provide food and company, but her constant talk of dying was draining. And there wasn't anyone else to help. Her mother and father were somewhere in Africa shooting one of their documentaries.

Joanna ambled into the kitchen and started cleaning up. Grandmother was probably worried that Matt might think she wasn't perfect housewife material, she thought wryly. She was funny that way. With all her insistence that her only grandchild go to college and get a good education, she nevertheless expected her to choose a career as a wife and mother as soon as she found a husband.

She wished again she'd asked Matt when he was likely to be here. With his busy existence, ASAP could mean anything from minutes to weeks.

After making sure everything was up to her grandmother's standard, Joanna hung around in the kitchen and living room, the two rooms facing the front of the house. She was hoping to catch Matt before he rang the doorbell and woke the old woman up. There were things he needed to know. She needed to talk to him before he talked to his godmother, explain why Grandma still didn't know.

Long before she had realistically expected him, his car was stopping in the driveway, headlights beating their way through the rain. Joanna's heart started pounding and she felt her palms dampen as she clenched her fists at her sides. He still had the same car. Of course, she should have expected it—it wasn't much over a month since she'd sat in that car herself, but somehow she'd expected things to change as much as her life had changed.

She stood in the shadow of the curtains by the window and watched him step out of the car. He glanced up at her grandmother's bedroom window as he slammed the door shut and strode toward the front door. He looked grim and tired.

Joanna opened the door, the darkness of the unlit foyer giving her some protection at least, and sent him a smile that was supposed to be cool and sophisticated, but somehow ended up wobbly and fake instead. Matt didn't smile, and she found herself missing the grin he'd usually greeted her with. He nodded curtly as he entered the house, his eyes raking over her once from the top of her head to her toes and back up.

"Hello, Jo," he said, unsmiling, and she stepped back, the shock of being so close to him again confusing her senses and making her head spin. The warmth of him almost seemed to reach out toward her and despite everything that had happened, the instinctive longing to step into his arms and feel them close around her was almost uncontrollable.

It was also hateful.

He hadn't changed since she'd seen him last. The dark hair, now glinting with raindrops, was the same. The green of his eyes was still hypnotizing, even when filled with fatigue and wariness instead of love and humor.

Of course he hadn't changed, she castigated herself. People didn't change in just a few weeks. Not unless some life-altering event happened to them, something that took their life, their existence, and turned it upside down.

Obviously, no such thing had happened to *him*.

Matt switched on the light and stared at her, his expression changing from serious to astonished. "You've changed, Jo." He took a deep breath and reached out toward her, only snatching his hand back when it was inches away from touching her hair. "What the *hell* did you do to your hair?"

He sounded furious. Joanna rubbed her temple self-consciously. Her hair was rather short now. In fact, Matt's hair was probably longer. She'd gotten carried away. So had her hairdresser, taking her cry of "I just want it gone!" a bit too seriously.

Matt's obsession with her hair was the reason she'd cut it, she knew that now that she was finally out of the denial stage...but leaving only a few inches had been a mistake. She looked like a shorn sheep.

She bit back the natural response: "It's none of your business," and tried for a cold smile and a neutral greeting instead. "Hi, Matthew. Good you could make it."

Matt's gaze was still on her hair, astonished and livid. He might not have loved her, but he had loved her hair. She straightened her back, suddenly very pleased with her new haircut.

His gaze slowly moved to her face again and his eyes narrowed as he shook his head. "You look like hell, Jo. You're thinner, too. Haven't you been eating?"

Was that guilt in his voice? Surprised guilt? Did he think she'd been pining away over him?

She'd ignore him. She'd ignore all personal comments he made and just focus on Grandma. "Thanks for coming, Matt," she managed to say amicably. "Grandma will be happy to see you."

Matt snapped out of his intense scrutiny of her and glanced toward the stairs. He pulled off his gloves and stuffed them in the pockets of his jacket, the anger finally fading from his eyes. "How is she?"

Jo shrugged. "She thinks she's dying," she said, disappointed to hear her voice break. "We don't know. She hasn't been getting out of bed much and she says she's weak, but then she isn't really sick either. She's an old woman." Breath left her in an involuntary sigh and she felt those nasty tears gather forces again. "The doctor says he sees no immediate problem, no reason to think she's really dying...but she's so sure that it's impossible not to worry..."

Matt reached for her, compassion in his eyes, but she flinched away. "She needed to see you," she said, gritting her teeth as she realized she'd wanted his touch. "That's why I called. She asked for you."

Matt headed for the stairs, without even removing his jacket. She grabbed his arm, the cool leather of his jacket familiar under her hand. "Wait. She's asleep now. And she isn't upstairs in her room, she's been staying in the downstairs guest room."

Matt paused and looked back. She released his arm. "She hasn't been sleeping well lately, so it's probably better if we let her sleep a bit. She has a bell, and will ring as soon as she needs anything." She paused. "Unless you're in a hurry to get back to work? If so, I suppose I could wake her up."

Matt shook his head and shrugged off his jacket. He tossed it over a chair and looked around. "No. I'm fine. I told people I had a family emergency and wouldn't be in for a while. I brought my laptop, so if you just have a kitchen chair and telephone line for me, I'll be fine for a few days."

A few days? She wouldn't survive several days with him in the house. "Matt, you don't have to *stay*. She just wanted to see you for a minute. She wants to talk to you about…"

Yes, Jo, a sarcastic voice whispered in her ear. *What is it she wants to talk to Matt about?*

Jo bit her lip. She had to tell Matt. She wasn't sure how she was going to tell him, but he had to know before he talked to her grandmother.

"…some things. Well, anyway, there are plenty of kitchen chairs." She led the way to the kitchen, where she had consumed untold gallons of coffee for the past couple of weeks. Somehow everything looked surreal with Matt at her side again. "Would you like some coffee? Or tea?" She knew he preferred coffee, knew how he liked his coffee, was familiar with the way he liked to stir it even though he never added sugar or cream, but they were strangers now. She was determined to keep it that way, to treat him like a stranger.

"Thanks. Coffee would be great."

She poured him a cup, put milk and sugar on the table, even though she knew he used neither, and sat opposite him at the kitchen table. She'd expected anger in his eyes, real anger, not the momentary fury of shock over her vanished hair. There had certainly been enough anger last time they'd seen each other. But now there was none. Just wariness in the way he looked at her, as if he wasn't sure what to expect. Somehow, the lack of anger was disappointing. He didn't care anymore—if he ever had, if it had ever been more than infatuation. The old woman napping in the guest room was now all they shared.

"Why is she staying in the guest room?"

"She suggested it herself. Going up and down the stairs was getting to be difficult for her, and she likes to be able to come to the dining room to eat."

Matt held his teaspoon between forefinger and middle finger and started work on creating a whirlpool in his mug. His eyes were steady on hers, too familiar and too alien, both at once. "Fill me in, Jo. What's wrong with her?"

Joanna shrugged. "We're not really sure what is wrong, except the big one: old age. I visit at least twice a month, and I started to notice about a month ago that she was a bit preoccupied and absent. I was worried, but her memory seemed to be functioning fine. But then for about two weeks now, she's been feeling very weak, and she hasn't wanted to get out of bed much. So I moved in for the time being. The doctor says he can't find anything specifically wrong with her, but at her age..." Joanna bowed her head and warmed her hands on her own cup. She wasn't ready to let Grandma go. Far from it. "We just don't know. She thinks she's dying. She's quite sure she only has a few days left. I don't know. At her age, people may sense these things. Be ready to go. The doctor says he's seen that before."

Matt put his elbows on the table and raked both hands through his hair as he stared into his coffee cup. "It's been months, hasn't it? I haven't seen her for months...not since we'd just started—"

"She asks a lot about you," Jo interrupted. "She keeps talking about you."

"She does?"

"Yes..." Joanna clenched her fists on the table. *Tell him!* she screamed at herself, but somehow she couldn't make herself do it. It was too complicated.

She didn't know how to explain her reasoning, how to make him understand how logical it had been at the time.

"Dammit," he swore. "I should have been there. I should have come to see her more often."

The soft jingle of the bell drifted into the kitchen, and before Joanna had even put down her mug, Matt was already out of the room.

"Matt! Wait. I need to tell you something…"

Too late. He had already vanished into her grandmother's room. Joanna pushed herself away from the table and ran after him, cursing her own cowardice.

Too late. From here on, it was all about damage control.

When she entered the room, Matt was bent over her grandmother, his arms around her. Grandma's beaming face was visible over his shoulder.

"Esther!" Matt said warmly. "It's been too long. You know how I tend to let the office swallow me up until I forget everything. You shouldn't let me get away with it."

Grandma smiled, blue eyes sparkling at the sight of her godson, but she didn't sit up, a depressing sign of her weakened state. "Until you forget everything? Not quite *everything*, I hope," she said, looking at Joanna with a grin. Matt glanced back too, his smile absent and his expression puzzled.

"I'll leave you two alone," Joanna said, all courage gone. It was too late even for damage control. She'd made a huge mistake. All she could do now was hope Matt caught on and didn't say anything to upset Grandma. "Just call me if you need anything."

"No, wait, Jo." Her grandmother's trembling hand

reached out toward her. "Don't go. I want you here as well. I need to talk to both of you."

Joanna hesitated, then came to her grandmother's side on the other side of the bed from Matt. She sat down on the edge of the bed. Matt pulled up a chair and sat down too, his hand in Esther's.

"So, how are you, old crone?" he asked, squeezing her hand. "You were still beating me at chess last time I saw you. What are you doing in bed this time of the day? Someone steal all your dresses from the clothesline?"

Joanna watched her grandmother's eyes brighten as the two of them began their usual banter. She should have called Matt sooner, she castigated herself. Grandma loved to see him, but didn't want to bother him much, despite all her cracks about curing him of his workaholism.

Grandma looked between them, smiling. "I'm so happy to have both of you here, finally. You see, I don't think it'll be long until I get to find out what the afterlife is all about." She shook her head when Matt started to protest. "Don't. I'm old and I'm tired. I'll be ready to go soon." She took a wheezing breath. "I have a request for you. Both of you."

"Anything," Matt muttered. "You know that, Esther. All you have to do is beckon and we jump."

Grandma's face creased in laughter, and her eyes were shining as she looked at Matt. "Good." She tightened her grip on their hands. "Because you see, I want you two to get married before I go."

CHAPTER TWO

JOANNA was still reeling over the content of her grandmother's words when she heard Matt give a shaky laugh. "Wow. Get married? You don't pull any punches, do you, Esther?" He glanced at Joanna, looking confused as well as shocked. In fact, he was looking as if he expected her to straighten this mess out.

Joanna opened her mouth, but only a squeak emerged, so she closed it and concentrated on trying to remember how her vocal chords worked. Her grandmother squeezed her hand, and she brought Jo's hand to meet Matt's on top of her duvet. His hand felt hot on top of hers, probably because her own was ice-cold, a familiar state since they'd broken up. She felt a jolt of recognition at his touch and gritted her teeth. This was no time to wallow in self-pity or a broken heart. This was about her grandmother who had the wrong idea.

A very wrong idea—and it was Jo's fault.

"I know it hasn't been long since you two discovered each other," he grandmother continued. "You're probably still keeping it a secret from most people, aren't you? But I've seen you together, I was in on it from the beginning, remember? No need to look so shocked."

Joanna felt her face grow red-hot as Matt's accusing gaze settled on her. Busted.

Grandma let go of their hands and cradled Matt's

hand in both of hers. "You understand, Matt, don't you? I need to see my little girl safe. She's never been able to count on her parents, and I couldn't bear to leave this world knowing I was leaving her behind all alone."

"Esther..." Matt said weakly. "Jo is not a 'little girl'. She's an adult. She's an independent woman with a career and her own life. She doesn't need a husband to be 'safe'. She can take care of herself."

"You're right, Matt. She doesn't need a husband. But she does need you." Grandma shook her head. "I know it's old-fashioned, but then I am a relic. I need this." She gave a weak wink. "You don't want me haunting this house and then roaming the earth for centuries, do you?"

"Grandma..." Joanna felt guilty about it, but anger stirred over her grandmother's scheming. "We can't. We're not ready. Please don't ask this of us."

Grandma sighed. "And here I thought an old woman would never be denied a deathbed wish."

If the knowledge that this could indeed be her grandmother's deathbed hadn't been at the forefront of her mind, Joanna would have rolled her eyes in exasperated recognition of her grandmother's manipulation. This was probably the geriatric equivalent of throwing a tantrum. "Grandma...you know I love you. I'd do almost anything for you." She shook her head. "But I won't get married just because you want me to."

Her grandmother took a shallow breath and blinked rapidly. "Don't say no right away, love. Think about it. At least sleep on it. Matt, what about you? You'll think about it, won't you? That's all I'm asking."

"Esther, nobody wants to be pushed into a marriage,'' Matt replied, and Joanna sighed in relief at hearing him approach this logically, yet kindly. He wasn't going to spill the beans. ''Besides, nothing will change. Our relationship won't change any by rushing into marriage.''

''It's already too late for me to see your children be born. I so want to know you'll be safe with each other before I leave. Marriage is a sanctuary, children. I know you love each other. If you get married I know you will always shelter each other. Matthew, I know you love Joanna. I know you'll always take care of her, but both of you need the safety that comes with complete commitment.''

His smile was sad. ''You know, Esther, there are no guarantees, even with love, and even within a marriage.'' He glanced at Jo. ''Sometimes your best just isn't good enough.''

''Don't say that, Matthew. You have to enter into this marriage with optimism.''

Matt shook his head and his tone hardened just a bit. ''Esther, please give this up. Joanna and I aren't ready for marriage yet.''

Despite the shock and sizzling anger over her grandmother's interference, Joanna winced at seeing disappointment darken the lined face. Her grandmother's health had been frail for weeks now. Originally there hadn't seemed any point in making her miserable by telling her that she and Matt had broken up—especially not when just the thought of having to explain the what and why had been so painful. It would have forced Esther to take sides, and Jo hadn't wanted that either. So, day after day, she'd postponed it. It had been easier to let her think they were still together, that the long evenings Jo sometimes had to spend at her new workplace were spent with Matt. She'd pushed that problem ahead of her, hoping....

She bit her lip—she'd hoped Matt would be the one to tell her grandmother they weren't seeing each other anymore. This was all his fault—why should she be the one to break an old woman's heart? Esther had been thrilled when her only granddaughter and her favorite godson had fallen in love—she would be devastated to hear they had broken up.

Of course, Matt didn't see Esther very often, so unlike Jo he hadn't had the opportunity to tell her anything.

Until now—and he couldn't be allowed to tell her now. Not when she was so weak. Would he understand?

She stole a glance at Matt, sitting there, his hand still in Esther's hand, his expression brooding, but the surprise had vanished already. At least he'd caught on. This was no time to dump the truth on Grandma, and he seemed to understand that. Her shoulders slumped in relief, even as she realized that her omission of truth was now digging them an even deeper hole.

Esther snorted. "Nobody's ever ready for marriage. Even when they think they are, they aren't."

"We're nowhere close to ready, Grandma. Neither of us is," Jo said, her voice clipped. She strove to add warmth to it—she didn't want Grandma to catch on to the truth after all. "Not now. Who knows what will happen later on." She almost grinned to herself as she caught Matt's surprised glance. If they really still were together, and in this predicament, she could just picture the panicked look on his face at hearing her voice the possibility of marriage.

She'd already been dreaming about forever-after, but she very much doubted he had. The closest he'd come to articulating feelings for her had been burrowing up to her, half-asleep, muttering that it was impossible to get close enough. It had warmed her heart at the time, making it leap in hope as she whispered "I love you" soundlessly against his skin, making sure he wouldn't hear it. Not yet. She'd never felt secure enough to say the words—not when he never came close to mentioning love himself.

And he never had.

"But it's so obvious that you two are in love," Esther said. She grinned, a teasing look on her face as she looked at Matt. "It's been obvious since that day just before Christmas when my granddaughter dropped by one evening, walking two feet above the ground with her skates around her neck and smiling so widely I worried that her face would split."

"Grandma…" Embarrassed, Joanna fiddled with her hair. A few weeks ago it had been long enough to provide a much-needed shelter to hide behind when she was blushing. But not anymore—three inches just wouldn't do. "Don't bring that up now…"

Grandma winked at Matt. "Could that have been a first-kiss day?"

Matt chuckled. Joanna heard the sound, and could imagine the grin that went with it. The grin that would have gone with it, she corrected herself, if theirs was still the relationship her grandmother thought it was. She didn't want to think about their first kiss, and she was sure Matt didn't want to either. She stole a look at him, and saw a faint smile as he held Esther's hand.

She took a deep breath. All she could do was pray Matt understood and would continue to keep up the act, at least until Esther was better. She wouldn't risk her grandmother's health on heartbreak.

Her grandmother's face sobered, and her thin hand tightened around Matt's. "Matthew, I don't have much time. I honestly don't think it'll be more than a few days now."

"Don't say that," Joanna chided her grandmother gently. "You're not going anywhere. We need you on our side for a while yet."

Grandma squeezed her hand. "I'm ready for the other side, love. But I don't want to leave you unless I know you're in good hands." She released Jo's hand and enveloped Matt's hand with both of hers. "Matthew, you were always a good boy, and you've grown into a fine man. Will you promise me that you will always look after my Joanna?"

Matt glanced up at Joanna, his expression unreadable. His gaze fell back on the frail old woman in the bed, and his smile was soft and gentle. His words were smooth, without hesitation, and they sliced Jo's heart. "I promise, Esther. I will look after Joanna the best I can."

Esther's sigh was wheezing. "It will have to be good enough, I suppose."

Joanna didn't speak as they left the room, just gestured for Matt to follow her to the kitchen to be sure they were out of her grandmother's hearing range. The old lady had intended to take a nap, but it wouldn't hurt to be on the safe side.

She walked into the kitchen, intending to sit down at the kitchen table, but felt too high-strung to stay in one place. She stood instead, motioning for Matt to sit down, but he declined, leaning against the kitchen counter instead, his arms crossed on his chest. He looked intimidating; his eyes boring into hers whenever she dared meet them. She gave a deep sigh. He wanted an explanation. And she owed him one. Or two. Or three.

Or did she? This was just as much his fault as it was hers. He was the one responsible for their breakup and if he'd visited his godmother more often, he could have been the one to tell her. Why should it have to be her responsibility when nothing of this whole mess was her fault?

"I suppose you have some sort of an explanation for this?"

Joanna rubbed her forehead, feeling exhausted. Too exhausted for a showdown. "Does it matter? I didn't know what she had in mind. I never dreamed she'd try to push us to get married."

"You know I'm not talking about that...marriage proposal." Matt shook his head. He got his laptop from his briefcase, plugged it in and connected it to the phone line as he spoke. Joanna felt a melancholy smile of exasperation tug at her lips. This too was familiar, the way Matt could work while he talked, while he ate, while he watched television. It didn't matter what he was doing, he could always give some portion of his attention to his work. It could be very irritating, but she'd been working on reforming him. One way she'd always managed to grab all his attention was by...

No. She bit her tongue hard and pinched her own arm for good measure. Compost heap again. Things sure seemed to ferment there.

"Let me summarize," Matt said, his voice dry.

"Esther still thinks we're madly in love, and is ecstatic at the thought of her two favorite people having found each other."

Jo gritted her teeth, unsure if what she was feeling was fury or fear. *Madly in love?* Was that just a sarcastic choice of phrase, or had he known about her feelings all along? "I know. I know, Matt, there's no need to rub it in."

And now it had gotten her in trouble. Matt in trouble. Both of them.

"You could at least have warned me," Matt said, still doing that infuriating trick of dividing his attention between her and his laptop. "You should have warned me that she didn't know. I nearly gave it away."

"Yes. I should have." Joanna paused, at a loss to explain why she hadn't done that, why she'd postponed telling Matt the truth until it was too late. "I guess I hoped the subject wouldn't even come up."

And look where it had got her. Her grandmother had proposed to Matt on her behalf.

Matt's laugh was short and harsh. His feelings were betrayed by the way he slammed the laptop shut. "I would say it did come up."

Joanna shook her head. "I would never have guessed she'd do that." She sighed, suddenly furious with herself. "I know it was cowardly of me, but I just couldn't tell her. At first I just wanted to wait until…" she broke off. There was no need to let Matt know precisely how crushed she'd been after their breakup, how the merest mention of his name had been enough to threaten tears flowing. "When her health declined, I didn't want to add to her worries. She adores you. She was so happy thinking we were seeing each other, and somehow it was never quite the right time to tell her."

She sighed, leaning her head against the wall, still not looking at Matt. "I couldn't bear to tell her, not even this afternoon when she demanded that I call you. I don't regret that—I'd rather pretend we're together than take any risks with Grandma's health. But I should have warned you—I'm sorry that I didn't."

Matt didn't reply. When she finally looked at him, he was staring out the window into the darkened garden, his brow heavy, lips tight. "You should have called me before. I had no idea she was so ill."

"She's getting on in years, Matt. What did you expect? It's not my role to make sure you spare the time to visit her."

"Spare the time?" Matt looked at her, then looked away and shook his head. He was silent for a while, then shrugged as he spoke again. "Well, you're right. I should have visited. But I would have appreciated a call to let me know she's failing."

Joanna clenched her fists and turned her attention away. "You're right, I should have let you know sooner. But that's irrelevant now. What are we going to do?"

"I don't know. She doesn't know anything about... what happened at work?"

Joanna straightened up and met his gaze directly. "No."

"She does know you switched jobs?"

"Yes. She thinks it's because the company enforces a strong policy against office relationships."

"It does have that policy."

"You think I don't know that, Matt?" They'd ignored that policy, which was the whole reason her entire future had nearly gone down the drain. Yes, she knew well enough about it.

"But she knows nothing else?" Matt asked.

"No. And we're not telling her. She thinks we're dating—and now she wants us to get married. That's all that matters now."

"I see."

"Do you?" she demanded. "She's old and weak. She thinks she's dying. She may be right. She's so happy thinking we are an item. She can be old-fashioned at times, but she worries about me and she thinks I'm safe with you."

"I see."

"Of course we're not getting married, but we can't ruin her illusion of us as a happy couple." Her mind was made up. They would keep up the pretence until Grandma was better. Or…until there was no longer a need for it. "Not now. You can't tell her we broke up."

He opened his mouth.

"Matt, say 'I see' one more time, and there will be no more coffee for you in this kitchen."

He looked at her in surprise, and then he smiled. His smile shot a flash of almost forgotten heat through her and she looked down into her coffee mug, trying to break the spell.

The doorbell rang, and she was grateful to escape. At the door, her grandmother's three bridge partners clustered on the top steps, and somehow the three five-foot-tall ladies managed between them to dwarf the tall elderly gentleman standing in the middle, looking rather shell-shocked.

"Anna, Rose, Nora," she acknowledged and stepped back. The old ladies filtered in, kissing her cheeks and chattering in a chorus. They visited her grandmother almost daily, and the laughter that filled the house during their visit, was probably better for Esther than all the doctors and medications in the world.

"Harlan Carlson," the man said, holding out a hand and smiling. He looked very distinguished with his silver hair and a neatly trimmed white beard, but not familiar. "I'm an old friend of your grandmother's. You must be little Joanna. We met many years ago, but you were very young, so you probably don't remember me."

Jo tried to place him, but with no luck. Her grandmother had so many old friends. "I'm afraid I don't," she replied apologetically, looking at the three ladies who were busy creating a mountain of outer garments after having piled their shopping bags in an equally impressive pile. Apparently they'd arrived directly from an extended visit to the mall. "But it's always a pleasure to meet my grandmother's friends, Mr. Carlson. Are you a new addition to the bridge club?"

His face creased in a hearty chuckle. "I don't think so. Esther called me a few days ago—I'm very much looking forward to seeing her again."

Joanna nodded, and beckoned him to follow as the three ladies filtered in a row toward Esther's room, talking loudly amongst themselves. Matt came out of the kitchen, shook hands with Mr. Carlson and was affectionately attacked by the three ladies. They followed the horde to her grandmother's room.

Esther was sitting up, almost bouncing at the sight of her friends filling the room. The air resounded with smacking kisses and fuss as everybody got comfortable at their usual stations. Mr. Carlson waited while the ladies got their greetings over with, and Matt leaned against the windowsill, his expression giving away nothing.

"Grandma?" Jo stood up on tiptoe and waved a hand to get her grandmother's attention over the crowd at her bedside. "Harlan Carlson is here to see you." She beckoned Mr. Carlson to step closer.

Grandma smiled and waved at him. "Harlan! It's been forever, hasn't it? I see your hair is turning white, just like mine."

"I'll bring up some coffee for your friends, Grandma," Jo said, and turned to leave the room.

"No—wait a minute, Joanna. It's because of you that I got Harlan here."

Jo turned around and squirmed between Nora and Rose to her grandmother's bedside, waiting for her grandmother's explanation. She was pretty sure this had something to do with dying. Was Mr. Carlson here to draw up a will, perhaps? She suppressed a sigh and a twinge of fear. "What do you mean?"

Grandma looked up at her, pleading in her eyes. "Harlan is a retired judge. He can marry you and Matt."

"What?"

"Please, Jo. Get married. Now. I know Matt will agree if you do. Harlan can marry you now." She reached up and stroked Jo's cheek. "You could be Mrs. Bentley in one hour, love."

Jo felt her insides heave. The silence in the room was deafening; even the bridge trio held their breath. "Grandma—you called for a *judge,* so he could marry me and Matt—here and now?"

An almost imperceptible nod, the look on the lined face a blend of guile and hope. "Harlan retired a while ago, but he can still perform weddings. Of course we don't have the paperwork, but...he's an old friend—I called in a favor.''

Mr. Carlson—*Justice* Carlson—cleared his throat. "This is very unusual," he said, looking between her and Matt. "I probably wouldn't be doing this for anyone except Esther, but I understand..." He hesitated, then shook his head. "Well, there is considerable urgency. You don't have a license, so you have to realize this is not a legal ceremony. You'll have to do this again officially, with the proper paperwork in order.''

Jo felt tears teeter at the corner of her eye. She blinked them away. This was funny, she told herself. She'd tell her friends about this next week, and they'd have a good laugh. "Grandma—I can't believe this! What happened to 'sleep on it'?''

"I was speaking rhetorically. You've had time to think about it.''

"Grandma, please. Don't do this. It's not right. Don't try to control our lives. Don't do this to us. I don't want to disappoint you, and neither does Matt, but we can't do something this drastic just because you want us to. Please, don't do this.''

Esther squeezed her hands together. "Forgive me, Joanna, but I must meddle. It means so much to me to see you marry Matt before I leave.''

"Justice Carlson just said, it wouldn't be legal, Grandma.''

The old lady waved away her objections. "Harlan can marry you now—to me that'll be just as valid as any other wedding. Then you'll just do it all over again with the paperwork and rice later. The important thing is that you make the commitment to each other, that you say the vows. That's all that matters. There's time enough for the petty details later. Time that I don't have," she added with a sigh.

"But it's not..."

Grandma didn't let her interrupt. "I know. You want a proposal from your man, not an old lady ordering him to marry you. But things are urgent now." She lifted a finger at Joanna and managed to wave it around without moving her hand. "I bet you would rather that I boss you around now than that I haunt you in the afterlife, wouldn't you?" She grinned, a lively spark in her eyes that belied a woman on her deathbed. "I haven't seen your grandfather in twenty-two years. We'll have better things to do than chase after you, rattling our chains."

Esther's friends cackled, and Joanna couldn't help but smile, even as tears continued to well in her eyes. This woman had been everything to her, a substitute for the parents that had never been there. "Don't worry about me, Grandma. I'll be fine. I don't need Matt to look after me, any more than he needs someone to look after him."

"Oh, he does, love. It's not just him who has to do all the work. You need to look after Matt for me. That's why I need you two to get married." A trembling hand reached out for the glass of water on the nightstand. "I'm afraid I don't have much energy. I think I need to rest soon again." A long time passed as she brought the glass to her mouth, drank, and put the glass back down. She was so weak now, Joanna thought in anguish. Just a couple of months ago she was walking the dogs by herself, and now she had to struggle for a drink of water.

"Tell me children, will you do this for me, let me

see you get married before I die?'' There was a des-
peration in her voice, hope in her eyes that cut Joanna
to the quick. She covered her face with her hands for
a minute, then dropped them, dejected. She took a
deep breath. Matt was standing silently by the window, arms crossed as he stared out into the evening
darkness. No help there.

There was no choice, was there? She'd have to tell
her the truth, hoping she could put it gently enough,
hoping her grandmother would understand, wouldn't
be too disappointed, wouldn't grieve too much for a
future her granddaughter and godson would not share.
She leaned forward and patted Esther's hand.
''Grandma... You don't understand... There's something you should know...'' She looked at Matt, pleading for assistance, but his profile was hard and distant.
She sighed and looked back at her grandmother.
''Grandma... We're not...''

Grandma waved a hand, dismissing her concerns.
''I know. The two of you haven't been together very
long. But I don't have time. It would mean everything
to me to see you safely together—and it's so obvious
that you belong together.''

Oh, God. How could she explain this? ''It's not...''

''Jo, could we speak outside for a moment?'' Matt
had turned around and was nodding toward the door.
''We'll be back in just a few minutes, Esther.''

Esther smiled. ''Take your time. I know my request
is a shock...'' She gestured weakly. ''It would just
mean so much to me. Discuss it. I'll just chat with
the girls and Harlan while you're talking. Take all the
time you need. We have all evening.''

All evening. Terrific.

Matt strode to the kitchen, his steps long and fast,

and he was already pouring more coffee into their mugs when Joanna reached the door.

He grabbed the mugs in one hand, sugar and milk in the other and flung himself into a kitchen chair, banging the two mugs on the table hard enough to splatter coffee on the wooden surface. He motioned her to sit down opposite him, and she reluctantly did so.

"She's bluffing, Jo. You've got to know she's trying to manipulate us."

"Of course she's trying to manipulate us! She wants us married before she dies, and she's not above using emotional blackmail."

"Are you sure things are that serious? She's looking well…" He shook his head. "I find it hard to believe she's really that sick."

"You haven't been here, Matt. You haven't watched her deteriorate. You didn't move her things to the downstairs bedroom because she could no longer master the stairs, you haven't been here to see her stop getting dressed in the morning."

"Have you called in a specialist to look at her?"

Jo shook her head. "You know how she is with doctors. It's good old Dr. Harrier or nobody."

"She *could* be lying to us."

"*Lying?*" He was dismissing her, dismissing her fears for Grandma, dismissing the old woman's frail health, and his callousness infuriated her. "How can you say that? Why would she lie to us about something so serious? Just to get us married, when she thinks we're heading that way anyway? If you're thinking about confronting her with that suspicion, forget it! She doesn't deserve being called a liar, just because it's convenient for you!"

Matt stared at her for a long moment, then looked down into his coffee. There was silence in the kitchen for a long time before he spoke again. "Okay. I'm sorry. You know the situation better than I do. I didn't mean to sound so harsh, but she seems fine to me— and we both know how she likes to meddle. But I suppose it's just wishful thinking on my part that she's actually faking." He took a deep breath. "Fine. We assume she's telling the truth. The way I see it, we have three choices. One—we can tell her we broke up. She'll be pretty devastated. Two—we can stick to our guns and tell her we're not ready to get married. The same there, she won't like it, and she may try to make us feel guilty, but she'll accept it sooner or later."

Neither option sounded appealing. "And the third?" she prompted, hoping Matt had come up with a magic solution that would fix everything.

"We can do what she wants and get married."

Joanna opened her mouth to reply, and shock started a coughing fit instead. It didn't subside until after she had taken long gulps of the glass of water Matt pressed into her hand to replace the coffee mug.

"Bad joke, Matt. Really bad one," she mumbled when she could speak again.

"It's probably the safest solution if you're worried about the shock to her health."

"What next? She'll ask us to have triplets, and we run straight to the fertility clinic?"

Matt stopped stirring his coffee and sent her a penetrating glance. "Jo, if you're right, and she really is dying, we're not going to get to do her any more favors, are we?"

Jo stopped breathing for a moment. It was one

thing to listen to her grandmother's proclamation of imminent death—she was used to that by now, although it hurt every time. It was something else entirely to have Matt say those words. "She can't die…" was all she could stutter.

Matt shook his head. "We can't know, Jo, we can only hope she'll be fine. But you're right, we owe her. If she really is sick and we can make her last days happy by pretending to get married, I'd say it's worth it."

"*Pretending* to get married? Are you suggesting we lie to an old woman on her deathbed?"

Matt shrugged impatiently, the simple gesture making her feel she was being unreasonable. "Does it matter? If I have a choice between lying to her or making her last days miserable, I'll go with the lie. What harm could it do?"

"I can't lie to her like that. I can't. And it would be too complicated. She'd want to attend the wedding." She shook her head. "And don't even say it. I'm not going through with a fake wedding."

"Jo, she knows a wedding here and now won't be a real, legal one. She brought her friend here without warning—she knows we don't have a license. She doesn't care about the legalities, for her it's the 'I do' in front of each other and witnesses that matters." He shook his head. "I'm not sure how she got a judge to agree to this, but Esther's always been good at manipulating people, hasn't she?"

Joanna stared at him, almost unable to believe he was really suggesting this. The idea was preposterous. It was out of the question.

She was still working on getting over Matt. Marrying him wouldn't help the healing process.

Yet, it was the easiest way out of this mess. Her grandmother would be happy, and there wasn't anything lost, was there? It was just one ceremony, some pretending. It wasn't as if this would be a real marriage.

Matt tilted the half-empty mug and pushed it back and forth on the table, his dark eyes weary. "Well? Shall we do it?"

He sounded as if he had just offered to have his head cut off. He wasn't any happier about this than she was, but that was beside the point. He was willing to make this sacrifice for Esther. Of course she was too.

Without realizing, her mind had been made up. She nodded. "Okay. I'll do it."

Matt nodded, his expression grim now. She stood up and occupied herself with making a fresh pot of coffee. Matt poured the remains of the old coffee into his mug, and she remembered how he didn't really mind—didn't really notice—whether coffee was scalding hot or tepid.

More memories from the compost heap. She didn't want to remember him and his coffee, or how he smiled when seeing her after a long separation, or how he kissed her absently when thinking about something else. Or the wrinkle that appeared between his eyes when he was talking on the phone, or the way he didn't get around to getting his hair cut until three weeks after it was beginning to irritate him.

How could she have gotten to know him so well in such a short time?

For a while, when he'd been a teenager and she'd been a child, he'd been her idol, although they hadn't often met. She'd bounced around him at the infrequent family gatherings, followed him everywhere. Matt had told her later that he'd looked at her almost as a cute—if annoying—puppy. Even when she was no longer a child, she'd followed in his footsteps and studied architecture herself—although following his lead hadn't been a conscious decision at the time.

Then, after she'd graduated, and spent six frustrating months trying to find a job, he'd given her one in his architectural firm. It had only been a favor to her grandmother, and the patronizing way he treated her had driven her up the wall for a few weeks. Until she'd finally exploded. She'd cornered him off in his office and confronted him, dragged him to her work station and demonstrated that she was highly capable and very much overqualified for what he had her doing.

He'd given her a promotion.

The next evening he'd called her at home, and she'd started stuttering when she realized he'd called to ask her out.

She'd refused, of course. She wouldn't date the boss. She wouldn't date her grandmother's godson either. Too complicated.

He'd seemed to agree. But then he'd gotten Grandma to ask them both over for dinner. He'd been fun and charming, the look in his eyes no longer indulgent, but something different—something dangerous and exciting. And then he'd stolen a chunk of her heart over a game of cards between the three of them.

And a few days later they'd gone on a date. Matt, Jo—and Grandma.

From then on, she was lost. Hopelessly.

"What's so funny?"

Jo felt the smile stretch her face as Matt's irritated

voice yanked her back to the present. She straightened up and the smile vanished in an instant. "I was thinking about our first date," she blurted out before she could stop herself.

Matt stared at her, the look on his face wary. No wonder. What reason could she have—now—to think back on their first date with a smile—and to tell him about it?

She needed to learn to keep her mouth shut.

"You mean when we went skating?" he asked.

Another sweet memory dragged forward to grate on her nerves. How could there be so many after a relationship that had lasted such a short time? "No. The very first one. When you took me and Grandma out to dinner and a movie. Very devious."

Matt's smile was fleeting, gone almost before it managed to bite at her heart. "You were stubborn. I was determined."

"Dating the boss is never a good idea—especially when it's against company policy."

Their eyes met. Matt nodded. "You're right. It isn't."

"How are things at work?" she asked deliberately. Better get it over with. It had immediate effect. Matt stiffened, then rubbed a hand over his eyes in a gesture of fatigue.

"Fine, I guess. More or less. Still working on…" He shook his head. "Doesn't matter. How's your new job?"

Joanna nodded. "It's fine."

"You're happy there?"

"It's great," she repeated. "As good as can be expected. Not my dream job, of course, and I could be making better use of my skills, but then beggars can't be choosers, can they?''

''You did have a choice.''

''I prefer to be independent and find my own job, even if it means sweeping the streets, rather than let you hide me away somewhere at a convenient distance like an eighteenth-century mistress.''

Matt stared at her. ''Eighteenth-century mistress?'' He shook his head and turned away. ''I'm not going through this again, Jo. Everything spun out of control. Can't we just put that aside for now?'' His look was wry. ''You've made it clear that you don't plan on forgiving *or* forgetting, but at least we should be able to be civil to each other for a...while. For Esther's sake.''

Jo bit her tongue and stared at the man she'd promised to marry. She forced herself to nod. ''Of course. For Grandma's sake.''

CHAPTER THREE

"Aren't you going to tell him he can kiss the bride?" Esther demanded. She'd gotten dressed for the occasion, and Matt had helped her to the living room, where the ceremony was performed.

Matt winced. The short ceremony had been difficult. Jo had trembled at his side—and she wasn't the type to tremble at anything. He had specifically asked Justice Carlson to skip the kissing part, but Esther wasn't about to be deterred.

He felt the tension radiate off Jo, heard her quick intake of breath at Esther's question. She looked like she was standing on the gallows, not in her grandmother's living room, which had been transformed by candles thanks to the Bridge Club. She was clutching the improvised bridal bouquet her grandmother had thrust into her hands—a hastily put together mixture of anything not wilted from Esther's vases. Her "I do" had been a less-than-enthusiastic groan. His own vows had been quiet and calm—but the feeling that had accompanied the words had been a surreal one— as if this was something that was meant to happen.

"Well?" Esther demanded. "A kiss for the bride?"

It was more than obvious that Jo had no interest in being the kissed bride, but they had ambled onto this stage, and there was no choice now but to complete the play.

He turned to her, tried a reassuring and apologetic

smile before planting a small kiss at the corner of her mouth, but she wasn't even meeting his eyes. Her lips were cold, that much he could tell, even though the kiss lasted hardly a microsecond. Not even long enough for her to manage to flinch away.

There was scattered applause, and some sniffling into four handkerchiefs. The four ladies had bickered a bit over which two of them should be on the groom's side, and which on the bride's side, but in the end the issue had been resolved relatively peacefully—with everyone sitting more or less in the middle.

At least no one was throwing rice.

Nora clapped her hands, drawing everyone's attention. "We brought some refreshments," she announced loudly. "Cookies and pies and even a cake. Only two-tiered, but it will do. We even have champagne. We'll set the table." She trotted off, followed by Anna and Rose.

They'd known, Matt thought, narrowing his eyes to glare at Esther. It was obvious. So obvious that he could hardly believe he and Jo had both been fooled. The devious old lady had planned this all out, and had invited her friends to the wedding, sure that he and Jo would give in. And she'd been right.

He stared at Esther, wondering if he was the only one who saw that cunning little smile. He was itching to confront her, but not now. As soon as the old lady showed signs of improvement—and he'd no doubt that would be soon—he would give her a piece of his mind. If, on the other hand, he was wrong, and she wasn't malingering—well, in that case he'd have no regrets over having made her last few days happy ones, no matter if it cost him and Jo some sleepless nights.

He couldn't blame only Esther, though. He'd gone through with this willingly enough. He hadn't even insisted on waiting a few days. He looked at Jo, her head bowed as she fiddled with her bouquet. Had he been so quick to agree to this entire thing because subconsciously he was looking for an excuse to get close to Jo again?

Maybe. But where would they go from here?

Jo's sigh wasn't loud, but it reached both him and Esther. His bride was pale and it didn't seem that she was looking forward to the impromptu wedding reception.

"Love, you don't look like a radiant bride," Esther said in a low voice. "I know this is sudden, but you were getting married eventually anyway. I know you love the man." Her gaze moved between "husband" and "wife". "Then there is...you two need a honeymoon..."

"We're not going anywhere until you're better, Grandma," Jo said, some color returning to her cheeks at last. At Esther's insistence that nobody got married in jeans, not even at a deathbed, Jo was wearing the antique wedding dress originally made for Esther's mother. It had hung at the back of the closet for over half a century, since Esther's own wedding.

They hadn't quite managed to iron out the wrinkles, and the dress was yellowed with age and smelled of mothballs, even with perfume sprayed on it, but Jo looked lovely, even pale and drawn as she was. He hadn't pictured her in a wedding gown before, their relationship hadn't progressed quite that far, but she looked as lovely as any man could want his bride to look. "There will be plenty of time for honeymoons when you're up and about again."

Esther smiled. "We'll talk about this later. But I have a surprise for you. Just a little something to make up for how abrupt your wedding is. I know this isn't what you'd have wanted for a wedding day."

Uh-oh, Matt thought, and from the look on Jo's face, her thoughts ran along a similar path. Surprises and Esther were not a good combination. "What is it, Esther?" he asked, bracing himself for the worst.

Esther smiled. "I would book you a honeymoon suite, but I don't think we're going to get one on such short notice."

"I'm not leaving you, Grandma," Jo said. "I'm afraid you're stuck with me as a permanent house-guest until you're feeling better."

"Go upstairs and take a look," Esther said mysteriously. "The room you've been staying in, Jo. Go take a look."

"Oh, Grandma, what have you done?" Jo wailed, and Matt poked her softly with his elbow in an attempt to remind her of her role.

Pain shot up his arm as his elbow connected with—concrete?

What *was* she wearing?

He put his hand on her waist, gingerly exploring the hard, bony structure with his fingers. For once, Jo didn't flinch away from his touch, and he assumed it was because she had to have lost all sensation in that part of her body. "What is this, a wedding dress or an exoskeleton?"

"It comes with a corset," Esther primly informed him. "Do not refer to your bride's dress as a bug's anatomy, Matthew. It's not flattering."

"That thing can't be comfortable."

"Women's clothes aren't meant to be comfortable, Matt," Jo said. "Emancipation hasn't gotten that far yet. Ever tried heels?"

"Er...no."

"You should. It's an experience."

"And I thought we had it bad enough with neckties," Matt muttered.

Esther was smiling at their exchange, but she kept glancing back toward the stairs, and he was reminded of whatever was up there.

"Why don't we go upstairs and see what Esther is talking about?" he suggested.

Jo nodded. Matt offered Esther his other arm and they made the laborious journey to the dining room where her friends were busy setting the table with the finest china. He left Esther at the head of the table, where she started barking out orders, and pulled Joanna with him toward the stairs. He looked back as they left the room, just in time to see Esther exchange a wink with one of her co-conspirators.

Yes, he was ninety-nine per cent sure she'd be back to her robust old self no later than tomorrow morning.

"You're a terrible actress, Jo," he said in a low voice as they mounted the stairs. "It's a wonder your grandmother is buying this at all."

"There is nothing to buy," she retorted. "She knows I didn't want to get married. She knows I'm just doing this for her."

"Not quite," Matt protested. "She thinks you just agreed to move the wedding forward a bit. She thinks we're madly in love and were planning to get married anyway."

"It's okay that she knows I'm not happy about this.

She's manipulating us. I want her to know this isn't what I wanted.''

''Fine. You can let her know this isn't the wedding of your dreams. But if you don't stop acting like a sacrificial virgin, that might be a clue to the fact that I'm the last man on earth you want to marry.''

Jo gave him a quick look, eyes narrowed, lips drawn together in a hard line. ''I'm doing my best. We pretended to get married. Now what?''

''I don't know. We play it by ear.''

Jo took a sudden deep breath—or as deep as that dress would allow—and stopped in the middle of the stairs. ''This was a stupid idea. I can't believe we actually went through with it.'' She groaned and grabbed the banister, pulling herself up the rest of the stairs. ''This was a mistake. We're in deeper trouble than before.''

''Maybe,'' Matt agreed. ''But we did it, and it's too late to back out now. Try to smile a bit.''

Jo reached her bedroom door ahead of him. She grabbed the doorknob and threw the door open, stalking in without even hesitating.

She stopped short, and even the back of her head told him of her shock. He stepped over the threshold himself, and found things to be worse than he'd imagined.

''Oh, no.'' Jo brought her hands to her face and turned slowly around, peeking between her fingers at their ''surprise''. ''Oh, no,'' she repeated.

''This is…very thoughtful of them,'' Matt murmured. The room had been transformed into something out of A Thousand and One Nights, with candles and flowers everywhere and soft music playing.

''Grandma…'' Jo groaned and slid down to sit on

the edge of the bed. She bent her head. "Does she really think we're going to have a blissful honeymoon up here while she's dying in her bed downstairs?"

Feeling her grief, and knowing he would feel the same if he believed what she did, he reached toward her in a gesture of sympathy, but snatched his hand back as he remembered the way she'd recoiled at his touch the last time. "Don't write her off yet. Did you see her just now? She doesn't look like someone who's dying. I wouldn't be surprised to see her pull out of this tomorrow, now that she's gotten what she wanted."

Her head snapped up and she stared at him, tears making her cheeks glisten and the ferocity in her gaze causing him to take a step back. "Don't you dare give me that now, Matt. It's too late for you to try to weasel out of this! This is hard on both on us, but we're doing this for Grandma. It's not as if I want to be married to you any more than you want to be married to me. So just shut up and stop accusing Grandma of malingering!" Her voice fell again and her shoulders slumped. "She might die any day now. She doesn't deserve our suspicions—not if there's a possibility that she's right."

Her shoulders were shaking again and the urge to hold her was getting stronger. He couldn't. She didn't want him to, and he had no right. She wouldn't listen to his reassurances—fine, that had to be her choice. She'd find out soon enough. Esther would probably be signing up for water ballet or horseback riding next week. "Jo, please don't cry. We'll get through this. Let's go downstairs and thank her. Then we'll eat our cake, drink our champagne and chat with the old ladies and then it's over."

His words seemed at least to pull Jo out of her misery for a moment.

"*Over?* She's expecting you to sleep in there!" Jo was pointing at her queen-sized bed, sprinkled with rose petals, scented candles crowding the nightstand. "She's expecting us to have a wedding night up here!" She stood up, pacing in agitation. "We've made a dreadful mistake."

Matt flipped the lights on to banish the romantic candle glow, and Jo blinked. There was a tear on her chin, a silver path showing its crooked route from the corner of her eye. He found himself longing to reach out and rescue the tear. His lips almost itched to kiss it away.

He thrust his hands in his pockets and looked away from temptation. "She doesn't have a spy inside your closet, Jo. We'll go downstairs and thank her, and since she's sleeping downstairs, I'll sleep in her room tonight. After that, we work something out. It won't be a problem."

Jo didn't answer. She shook her head and left the room.

What a mess. Matt cast one last glance at the bed before leaving. Rose petals? A basket of God-knows-what on the bedside table?

He shook his head as he followed Jo back downstairs. Those old ladies had to have been reading something more risqué than *Reader's Digest*.

"Did you like what they did to the room?"

"It's lovely, Grandma." One truth among a plethora of lies. The room *was* lovely. She didn't know if she could bear sleeping in there tonight, alone. It seemed such a waste.

"I didn't go upstairs myself, but the girls described everything to me. They had some brilliant ideas. You know, Joanna," she mused, "between the four of us, we've got over 350 years. Quite a lot of living."

Jo was used to hearing her grandmother refer to her eighty-something buddies as 'the girls,' and the thought of the three sneaking old biddies arranging flowers and candles and putting satin sheets on her bed wasn't too absurd. They'd done worse.

"Everything's just lovely, Grandma." She bent down to hug the old woman and kissed her cheek. "Thank you. I love it."

"Did Matt like it, love? Men don't always appreciate romance."

"Matt loves it," Matt said, coming up behind them. "Thank you, Esther."

"It's the least I can do. I'm pushing you. I know. And depriving you of a proper wedding and a honeymoon. But I feel much better," she added. "Knowing the two of you will be together, I feel much better."

"Do you?" Matt's suspicions were contagious, despite her own conviction that Grandma couldn't possibly have the motivation to pull something like this off on a lie. For one thing, Esther hadn't mentioned dying at all in the half hour since the ceremony. Considering the frequency of death talk before, this was an unusually long reprieve.

"I do. I know you'll be safe with each other, and that's such a relief." Grandma was sitting at the head of the table, and she patted the tablecloth at each side. "Sit down. Have some cake. It's a bit squashed from being carted across town, but the taste hasn't changed."

Matt held the chair out for Jo, and helped her sit without too much damage to the gown. "You mean you didn't wait for us to cut the cake?" he asked. Grandma's hand paused on its way to her mouth.

"We forgot," she said. "We were hungry after all the excitement and we thought you two might be too busy…counting rose petals. Oh no." She peered over the table and her face brightened. "There's an untouched pecan pie. Maybe you could cut that instead?"

Matt reached for the pecan pie and put it in front of Jo. He grabbed a knife and put it in Jo's hand, and enveloped it with his own. Heat shot up her arm, and suddenly it wasn't only the corset that was constricting her breathing. His other hand was on her shoulder, and she felt the touch all over.

Why was he doing this? she thought in distress. Nobody had even suggested they cut the cake—the pie—together. He took this charade far too seriously.

He took his duty to Esther seriously. Of course he did. So should she. Bravely she raised her head and smiled up at him, even though it hurt her cheeks.

Jo picked at her cake and pie and sipped the champagne without noticing any taste. She was married to Matt, and he was sitting across the table, eating a squashed wedding cake and chatting with Grandma and her bridge club. The marriage wasn't legally binding, and no documents had been signed, but she felt married. The plain band on her finger—another item Grandma's buddies had just happened to bring over—felt real and heavy despite its slimness.

Yes. She felt married. And when this was over, she'd probably feel divorced.

What a mess.

Matt was handling this much better than she was, laughing as he chatted to Esther and her friends, and he had enough of an appetite to sample each of the three pies they'd brought. He acted as though pretending to get married was something he did every day, Jo thought irritably. It didn't hurt him as it was hurting her, but then he'd probably never spent their nights together staring at her face, wondering what she'd look like on their wedding day. They'd only been together a couple of months, but she'd already been having silly fantasies about them getting married. It had never been mentioned, of course. Much, much too soon for that, but she'd already secretly been dreaming of a church wedding and the way Matt would look in a tux.

She'd been so silly. So *young*—only a few weeks ago.

It was already getting late, and the bridge trio sampled each other's pies relatively quickly and left, along with Justice Carlson. Esther also retired to her room, after giving them both a hug and a kiss, and something that Jo refused to believe had been a wink.

Then they were alone, sitting on opposite sides of the table, and the house was so quiet.

"Well," Matt said, bracing his elbows on the table and staring across to her. "It's over."

"Over? It's only just beginning," Jo snapped back at him.

There was silence. Matt was swirling the inch of champagne left in his glass and studying the sheen it left on the inside as if it held the key to the secrets of existence. "This is weird, isn't it?" he asked unexpectedly and looked up. "It feels weird. Like we really did get married."

Jo nodded. "Yeah. It is." That probably meant he was feeling trapped and cornered. Well, good. He deserved it. This was all his fault. She'd never even have considered going through with this if he hadn't planted the idea in her mind, if he hadn't made it look like the simplest, easiest, most humane way out of the tight spot Grandma had thrown them into.

She couldn't define her own feelings. They'd been drowned in a burning concern for Esther—and she had no idea right now how she felt about Matt. He still hadn't apologized for what he'd done to her. He didn't even seem sorry.

"Will you be okay?" Matt asked. He was looking concerned, and for some reason that made her furious. Where had his concern been before?

"Of course I will be okay, Matt. I was okay when you threw me out of your life and your company, wasn't I? If I can handle getting dumped and fired the same day, my reputation and my career trampled on by the man I was falling in love with—I can handle one stupid pretend marriage."

Matt's eyes closed and he looked tired. "Jo…"

"Forget it, Matt. Don't tell me once more that there was nothing else you could have done. It's over. Ancient history." Jo started clearing the table, avoiding Matt's look. The anger hadn't left her, it seemed. It had been simmering, waiting for the right moment to erupt. She'd regained control of her temper just in time, but nevertheless the china made alarming noises as her trembling hands stacked the pieces together.

"Don't do this now," he said at last, stopping her as she tried to take his plate away. "Your grandmother won't be pleased if you break her best china or get stains on that gown. We'll clean up tomorrow."

"I'm working tomorrow," she barked. "If this doesn't get cleaned up now, my grandmother will try to do it, and she's not strong enough."

"I'm not working tomorrow. I already said I'd be away a few days. I'll clean this up in the morning."

Jo dropped the plates back on the table. "Great. Far be it from me to object when a man offers to clean. So you'll be staying here tonight?"

"There is no choice, is there?"

"I suppose there isn't." She headed for the stairs. "Grandmother is in the guest room, so you'll have to take her room. The linen's in the closet. Good night."

"Night."

Jo had just managed to calm down enough to untangle herself from the straitjacket of a wedding gown and throw on a robe in preparation for a shower, when there was a knock on her door.

"Where did you say the sheets were?" Matt asked when she opened the door a scant inch. He'd rolled up his sleeves and unbuttoned his shirt and the sight stabbed her in the heart again. She hadn't seen him so casually dressed since before they'd broken up. It felt far too intimate now.

"In the closet closest to the window," she replied and started to pull the door shut.

"There's nothing there. The shelves are empty."

"The bed linen is right there, Matt. Three full shelves of it." Jo sighed, and stomped to his room. Men! When it came to finding things in closets, cupboards and refrigerators, their IQ was on a level with single-cell organisms. It was cute when you were in love and had your head in the clouds—but at other times it could be damned annoying.

But in this case he was right. The three shelves

usually filled with bed linen and extra blankets were all empty. She stood on tiptoe to peer at the back of the top shelf. "I don't understand. Could Grandma have lent them to someone?" She shrugged and turned away, walking straight into Matt's chest. She scurried back, then squeezed past him as he didn't seem about to move out of her way. "I'll just get you some from the closet in my room, then."

She threw her closet door open and reached up to fetch the linens.

Nothing.

"I don't understand," she said with a frown, pulling the other closet doors open to check, just in case. "All the sheets are gone."

"Laundry?" Matt suggested.

Jo shook her head. "No. I changed the beds last Wednesday, and there was a whole pile of linen in both closets back then. Grandma owns enough bed linen for a whole army."

"She must have moved them, or lent them. Or the bridge ladies did, when they came up here to change our... *your* bed."

Jo nodded. "I don't know why, or where they might have put them though. I'll go ask Grandma. She's probably still awake, she likes to watch late-night movies on television." She shuffled past Matt again—why was he always in her way?—and started heading downstairs.

"Yeah. That's a good idea, Jo." Matt's voice floated to her as she was halfway down the stairs. "Tell her we won't be sharing a bed on our wedding night, and therefore need more sheets."

She stopped. "Dammit."

"Yeah." She looked up to find him standing at the

banister, peering down at her. "I guess we could always tell her we didn't feel like sleeping on rose petals."

She ignored him. "There's a blanket downstairs on the sofa," she said, shuffling back up the stairs and tightening the belt on her robe. She didn't like the thought of Matt sleeping under her favorite comforter—it would probably never feel the same to her—but it was the only thing that came to mind. "It's only four feet long, and not very thick, but it's the only thing I can think of for you to use tonight."

Matt grimaced, and she remembered how he liked to huddle under the covers, using every inch of their length, pulling her into the curve of his body, his arm like a vise around her waist, even when he was fast asleep. He radiated warmth like nothing else on the planet.

"What about a sleeping bag?" he asked, hurtling her out of the memory.

"Maybe," she managed to get out, despite the lump in her throat. "There might be one up in the attic." She climbed the rest of the stairs and gestured at the ceiling where the hatch was. "The attic is up there, but I've no idea where Grandma keeps a flashlight. I don't feel like crawling up there with only a scented candle as a light source, do you?"

Matt shook his head. "The blanket will do. Good night."

"Night."

Jo shut the bathroom door before the echo of that single word had died out. She took a quick shower, then pulled on a ratty old nightgown she'd dredged up from the bottom of a shelf, something that definitely didn't belong on anyone's wedding night.

When she returned to her darkened room, the scent of the candles still permeated the air, and she opened her window wider to get rid of the smell. The soft moonlight spilled onto the bed, glistening on the sheets. Satin. She didn't think she'd ever slept on satin before.

Probably slippery.

She brushed the rose petals together and held them for a while in her cupped hands, close to her face.

They smelled lovely. Far too lovely.

She grabbed her jewelry box off the dresser and let the petals filter between her fingers and settle on top of the contents. They looked beautiful against the silk, with the sparkle of her silver things peeking through. She left the box open on the nightstand and crawled into the satin sheets. They were cool—and very slippery—but warmed quickly against her skin. She pulled the duvet up to her neck and buried her face in the pillow, feeling a sense of relief. Finally the day was over, and she had survived.

Even though she'd not only had to see Matt again, but had had to marry him.

The feelings that had swamped her the moment she'd heard his voice on the phone had only been reinforced by seeing him again. She wasn't over him yet. The anger was still there, the hurt—but also feelings for him, an attraction that hadn't faded at all during their weeks apart, and the aching realization of how much she'd missed him—something the bitterness had concealed from her before.

Maybe time did heal—but it sure didn't hurry.

Her last action, as usual for the past couple of weeks, was to check if the electronic bell was on. If

Grandma needed her in the middle of the night, she was only a few seconds away, one push of a button.

The sweet scent of the rose petals tantalized her nose, and she reached out and slammed the box shut. Her last half-crazed thought before exhaustion disintegrated into sleep was, that if she'd nothing else to show for her wedding night, at least she'd have sweet-smelling jewelry.

CHAPTER FOUR

Jo had cut her hair.

Somehow that single fact had wriggled through everything else, and disturbed his dreams all through the night, never mind small things like a fake wedding ceremony, a pretend marriage and all the complications that came with it.

Jo's hair was gone, the gorgeous soft mane that he'd so loved to bury his hands in. Her hair was almost shorter than his now.

It would grow again, he reminded himself as he settled in to work at the kitchen table, trying to squash that ridiculous—but nonetheless overwhelming—sensation of loss. Her hair wasn't gone for good. It would grow back, just as long and thick and beautiful.

If she wanted it to.

His "wedding night" hadn't been a very comfortable one. The blanket was too short, Esther's bed unfamiliar—and Jo's picture was on the nightstand. It seemed to have been perfectly placed so that her smiling eyes sparkled in the faint glow from the moon peeking in through the curtains. Even after the moonlight was no longer toying with him, he'd spent a big part of the night staring at her face, relaxed in laughter. It had been a while since he'd seen anything other than anger and distrust in her eyes.

Seeing her again had been a shock. He'd expected that—expected a jolt of sadness or anger—but he hadn't been prepared for an onslaught of guilt and a return of that fierce protective instinct that had been one of the most surprising aspects of his feelings for her before.

Why guilt? He'd done his best—he had nothing to feel guilty about. It had been her choice not to accept his help, her choice not to trust him when he promised to do his best to fix a very sticky situation. She hadn't wanted his protection—hadn't wanted *him*.

The feelings were there, nevertheless. Guilt, a longing to protect…and a resurgence of the emotions that had exploded between them during the short weeks of their relationship.

No, he admitted to himself. It wasn't over. He was just as hooked as he'd ever been—which was probably the real reason he'd gone through with the marriage ceremony despite his suspicions about Esther. Jo was worth fighting for, and he would fight if that was what it took.

She looked different now. Not only her hair—although just that had punched him in the gut the moment he'd seen her—but she was thinner, looking tired. Maybe the new job wasn't agreeing with her. Maybe Carl was driving her too hard.

His cell phone was in his hand before he'd consciously made a move to get it, but he shoved it back into his pocket with a decisive move. This wasn't any of his business. Jo wasn't his protégée—she could take care of herself. He'd already interfered more than she wanted him to—she was on her own now.

He rubbed the wedding ring, for a moment absently thinking that he had to get them real rings—not props borrowed from the bridge trio. He shook his head, irritated at himself. Was he getting dragged into Esther's fantasy of happily ever after? Of course he wouldn't be getting real rings—not any time soon, anyway. This wasn't a real marriage.

Or rather it wasn't a fully legal marriage—but that wedding band on his finger felt real enough. And now that the urgency of yesterday had met the cold logic of morning, his conviction that they'd been tricked had been confirmed. Esther wasn't dying—thank God. She'd been bouncing with energy this morning, so pleased with herself that he'd almost confronted her, almost demanded to know how she could do something like exaggerate her bad health in order to make them get married.

But that would have to wait. He had other plans.

He just wasn't sure they would work. Jo was among the most stubborn creatures in the universe.

Matt sighed as he started tapping on his keyboard, almost eager to escape into work, a few hours' distraction from the current dilemma.

Esther was still in bed with her puzzle books. He'd spoiled her with breakfast in bed and helped her out with a few tricky crossword problems. The old lady was looking very chirpy this morning, and seemed to be calling off her bluff already. She hadn't even mentioned dying today. After grumbling a bit that he should be bringing his bride breakfast in bed, and not an old crone, she'd asked him how he liked being a married man.

The question had come as a bit of a shock—his wedding band seemed tighter in the light of day, even knowing it wasn't official, no papers had been signed, and the bride most definitely hadn't put her heart in her "I do."

And now what?

His fingers slowed on the keyboard, and the diagrams on the screen blurred as he pictured Jo's laughing face, her hair spread over his pillow, her cheeks flushed with excitement and joy.

No, it wasn't over.

This was his opportunity, a blessing in disguise after all, a second chance.

The last month had been hell, on all fronts. He'd tried to do his best, for all people concerned, but he'd ended up losing Jo and risking his own position as CEO, in one glorious package. The theft of documents hadn't been a particularly serious incident in itself—but the uproar it had caused in the firm was the serious part, as it had to have been an inside job.

Jo and the board of directors had been a particularly nasty rock and a hard place. But this would be over soon. The investigation would come to an end. Jo's name would be cleared—he had no doubt about that, and he would regain the trust of the directors—including his father. Or so he hoped.

But Jo had never believed that he trusted her. When he'd tried to protect her, she'd taken that as an accusation, she'd refused to cooperate and left the position he'd fought so hard for her to keep, leaving both of them looking bad. That had made his struggle even harder—and yes, he'd been angry at her. But perhaps it had been partly his fault. In his fervor to make things right, to protect Jo, he'd kept her out of the decision-making—out of the know, even. He'd just wanted her to cooperate while he worked to fix things. In retrospect, that was probably a mistake. Now that his anger had faded, he could see her point of view, understand why she'd assumed he thought she was guilty—but it still hurt that she hadn't trusted him.

He was certain he'd soon regain the trust of the board, and then everything would go back to normal at the firm. His personal life, however, was a different story.

He sighed, losing his concentration completely as his eyes caught on Jo's bridal bouquet sitting on the dining-room table. Someone had shoved it into a small crystal bowl. The blossoms hung forlornly off the edge, petals trailing on the tablecloth. There was water in the bowl, but the flowers were already wilting. Of course, they hadn't been new yesterday when they'd been transformed from sickbed flowers to wedding flowers. Even he could see the colors and types were mismatched.

But they were beautiful nevertheless, and it was sad to see them wilting already.

Not that he usually cared when or if flowers wilted.

Without quite knowing why, Matt stood up, crossed the room and lifted the flowers out of the water, unraveling the white strip of material that had been wound around the stems, and that was now soaked in water. He squeezed most of the water out of the wet ribbon and wound it around his hand like a bandage. It looked like silk.

"It's one of Joanna's old hair ribbons."

"Huh?" Matt whirled around and came face to face with Esther. She nodded at the ribbon in his hand.

"The ribbon. It's Joanna's. A lot of her old things are here. You know, when she was a little girl, she often stayed with me when her parents were away."

"I know," Matt said dryly. He also knew that a more accurate statement would have been that Jo occasionally visited her parents when they could spare the time to have the inconvenience of a child hanging around.

"This was her favorite ribbon when she was eight years old. She always said it made her feel like a princess." Esther sank down in an easy chair, and spread a comforter over her legs. She sent him a penetrating glance. "That's what a woman needs on her wedding day, Matthew. She needs to feel like a princess."

Jo had looked like a princess in the antique wedding gown—but he didn't think she'd felt much like one. Unless it was a princess about to be locked in a tower—a princess without long hair.

First flowers, now fairy tales.

Who had been messing with his head?

Three guesses, Matthew, an inner voice commented with just the slightest touch of sarcasm.

"She made a beautiful bride, don't you think?" Esther sighed. "Lovely. A shame about her hair though."

"Yes," he agreed wholeheartedly, and Esther turned her head to fix him with her stare.

"Why did she cut it like that?"

He shrugged, and started unwinding the ribbon from his hand. "I don't know. Fashion? Short hair is probably in right now."

Esther snorted. "Fashion? Not good enough. Do you like her hair like that?"

"Jo is always beautiful."

"You hate it."

He chuckled. "Yes, Esther. I hate it."

"Good. Then maybe she'll let it grow back. For you." She reached for the phone on the table and gave him a haughty look. "Don't you have work?

Dishes to do? I've got phone calls to make, things to do.''

He grinned and saluted her. ''Yes, ma'am. I'll be in the kitchen if you need me.'' He held out the damp silk ribbon. ''Where should I put this?''

Esther stared into his hand for a moment, then her gaze flickered up to his face. ''Keep it, Matthew. You never know when a silk ribbon might come in handy.''

Jo couldn't reach her grandmother all day. The phone was constantly busy—Matt was probably online, working. She slammed the phone down one more time, and glanced at the clock. Still a couple of hours before she could leave. She considered explaining to her boss that she needed to take the afternoon off, but reluctantly dismissed the idea. She was overreacting. Grandma was fine. She was with Matt.

Besides, she'd been unbelievably lucky to get a job so soon after being kicked out of Matt's company, but she'd only been here for a month and however nice her new boss was, she couldn't afford to take any chances.

However, being cut off from the chance to check up on Grandma in her current condition was intolerable. She'd stop by on the way home and buy Esther a cell phone. If Matt was really going to be staying for a few days, this wouldn't do at all.

She could call him on his cell phone, of course, but she'd rather not. Not unless there was a serious urgency to reach Esther, and there wasn't. Not when he was there, at Esther's beck and call. There was no need for Jo to worry in the first place. She knew Matt well enough to know that he'd call her the moment Esther had any problem.

But worrying had become a habit in the last few weeks. She groaned and rested her head in her hands for a moment.

She'd always had trouble breaking bad habits.

By concentrating on work, she forced herself to stop calling, but left the office the minute the clock told her she could decently get away with it. There would be one stop on the way. Grandma would enter the twenty-first century, whether she liked it or not. She would soon be the proud new owner of a state-of-the-art cell phone.

Matt's car was still parked outside the house. He'd probably not moved away from the house all day, been tied to his computer. She dithered for a while in the car, postponing going inside.

They were married. Not legally, not binding—but as far as Grandma was concerned they were married, and they would have to act accordingly when Esther was around. Only a few weeks ago, marriage to Matt would have been a dream come true. Now—it wasn't.

She dug into her purse, finding the wedding ring she'd pushed into a corner at the very bottom, and slid it on. It seemed to weigh much more than any normal ring should, she thought, disgruntled, staring at it. How did Matt feel about wearing a wedding band? Did it make him feel tied down, as though he was choking? Or didn't he care at all, knowing it was all just temporary playacting?

She smirked as she pushed the door open, thinking about the dirty dishes they'd left behind last night. She hadn't lived with Matt, but they'd spent enough time together at his apartment for her to know housework wasn't his favorite chore any more than it was hers. It was unlikely that he'd actually done the dishes. She just hoped he hadn't allowed Esther to do them.

Esther was fully dressed, for the first time in over a week, and sitting at the dining-room table, working on a jigsaw puzzle. Matt sat opposite her, his laptop humming, and he was stabbing at the keys with one hand, while holding a cell phone to his ear with the other.

Typical Matt.

Esther smiled. "Welcome home, Joanna."

"I tried to call all day," she told Esther, and sent Matt a nasty look. "But the phone was busy." She moved to her grandmother's side, and put the brand-new cell phone on the table. "There. It's best if you carry it in your pocket. That way I can always reach you, and you can call whenever you need me."

"Another phone?"

"Matt's using the phone line," she explained. "So I couldn't get through. This way, I can reach you even if the phone line is tied up."

Esther examined the phone. "Good. I can chat while walking the dogs. Not bad. But Matthew wasn't on the phone, I was. I've been telling everybody about the wedding!"

Jo felt her heart drop to the pit of her stomach. Did Grandma mean... "You were telling—"

"Everybody," Esther repeated, beaming. "Well— except your parents, of course, I don't even know which continent they're on right now." She examined her new phone, still smiling. "It took me all day, but I've reached almost everyone. It's amazing how big the extended family is when you're my age. Granted, you may not know any of your cousins when you pass them on the street, but they're your blood. Matthew's mother was especially thrilled.''

Jo leaned back against the wall. She looked at Matt, but he was staring at his screen, his jaw clenched, looking as if he were determined to ignore the conversation no matter what.

''Grandma...please tell me you didn't call Matt's mother...''

''She told me you two hadn't even met, not since you were a child.''

''Oh, my God...''

''Remiss of you, Matthew. She's coming to town next month, just to meet you, Joanna.''

''What?'' Jo almost yelled. ''His mother? Here?''

Esther cackled. ''Matthew's responses were about the same. I understand about the nerves, but there's nothing to be worried about. Jane is a lovely woman. You remember her, don't you? You have a wonderful mother-in-law.''

''Mother-in-law...''

''Mothers-in-law aren't that bad. Really. Not as long as you treat their sons right.''

''Oh, God.''

''Don't be nervous, dear, she's just stopping by for a weekend. Just a casual visit. It's not as though we have to arrange a dinner party for fifty. Relax.''

''Relax?''

''Of course,'' Esther mused, ''we do owe people a proper wedding reception, don't we? Perhaps you two would like to repeat your vows in a church?''

''Grandmother!''

''Esther!''

Their admonitions formed a shocked and angry

chorus, even hurtling Matt out of his catatonic state at the computer. Esther grinned. ''Just a thought, children, just a thought. No hurry. I'm sure you'll want a real ceremony sometime, but there's no hurry.''

Jo shook her head and stalked away into the kitchen, irritated and annoyed at the entire universe—and more than a little upset.

As she'd guessed, the dishes were stacked in the sink, unwashed. She gritted her teeth and turned on the water, squirting liquid soap over the dishes. Men! Grandmothers! She wasn't sure which was worse.

''Leave them.'' Matt was standing right behind her and she jumped, almost screaming. He put his hand on her shoulder, steadying her, and she recoiled, turning around to face him, hand clenching the end of the counter. He tucked his hand in his pocket and shrugged, as if in an apology for touching her.

''Matt, your mother is coming. Did you hear? Your mother is coming to meet me! Oh, and why don't we just have a church wedding? She tricked us, didn't she? I bet she's been planning this for weeks. I bet her health was never failing at all. I bet tomorrow she'll be taking her usual walk around the block with the dogs, the way she used to do every morning.''

''That pretty much sums up what I suggested yesterday,'' Matt said dryly. ''And you bit my head off for it. But to look on the bright side, at least she's not dying.''

The wind went out of Jo. ''That's wonderful. I didn't mean…''

''I know what you meant.''

''We should tell her exactly what we think of her interference.'' Jo turned on her heel to do precisely that, but Matt grabbed her arm.

"Are you sure? She may have pushed us to get married before we were ready, but she did think we were a couple. She'll no doubt be pretty devastated to find out differently. Can we take that risk now?"

"But you know she's fine. Don't you? You've been saying that all along!"

"We can't be sure. It's probably safer to assume she's been telling the truth."

"So we don't confront her?"

"Not yet."

Jo rubbed her forehead, feeling tired already. Duplicity was exhausting. She wondered how Esther did it—if that was what she was doing. Matt was right. They couldn't be sure. "What's the alternative? To keep pretending?"

His shoulders lifted in a weary shrug. "I suggest we stick it out for a few days at least—play it by ear. The news is already all over town. We'd make Esther look like a fool, coming out with the truth now that she's told everybody that we're married."

Jo sagged against the counter. "Instead, we'll be the fools. I forgot. Everybody knows. Your mother knows. Your mother is coming to meet me." Everything was suddenly overwhelming, and dizziness swamped her. She felt Matt's hand on her shoulder.

"Jo? You okay?"

"Yeah." She straightened up, now furious with herself for displaying weakness. "I'm fine. I was just dizzy for a minute. Everything's so weird."

"Don't worry about my mother. That's next month—we'll probably have figured something out by then."

"Figure something out," she muttered. "That's

how this whole thing started, wasn't it? We jumped into this with our eyes closed to what a big mess we were creating, sure we'd 'figure something out'.'' She turned back to the sink to get Matt's hand off her shoulder, and grabbed the brush for some forceful dishwashing.

"Leave the dishes," Matt said again. "We've got plenty for tonight's dinner."

"Leave them?" she repeated. "Forever? I know it is hard for men to grasp, but these things don't get clean by themselves, however long you give them. Well, unless there's a dog in the house, and your definition of clean is flexible." She made an attempt at stabbing him with her glare, ignoring the fact that she had to be sounding like a bad-tempered witch. "Last night you said you'd do the dishes. You didn't keep your word."

"I know. I will. I bought a dishwasher. It should be here within the hour."

"A dishwasher?"

"Yes."

"You bought a dishwasher, just so you wouldn't have to wash a few measly dishes?"

"I bought a dishwasher so that Esther wouldn't have to worry about that chore in the future," Matt said with exaggerated patience that infuriated her.

"She doesn't do the dishes. Not while she's sick and I'm staying with her."

He shrugged, unconcerned. "Whatever. The dishwasher will be here soon."

Jo bit back a scathing remark about men and the lengths they'd go to in order to avoid housework. She'd just sound like a shrew, and she wasn't.

Not normally, anyway.

"Where will you put it? There isn't room for it."

Matt pointed. "We can easily remove that cupboard. It fits there. Esther has already approved it."

"And what do we do with all the stuff in there?" Matt stared at her, and she looked away. She was being unreasonable about a tiny issue. She knew that. It was a nice way not to think about the big issues.

She shrugged. "Fine. We'll find a place for the stuff." She folded her arms on her chest. "Matt, this has gone way out of hand. Why didn't you stop her from calling everybody?"

"Do you think I willingly let her make those calls? To my mother and my grandmother?" He swore. "I didn't know until my mother called me on my cell phone, screaming with joy and fury at the same time."

"Fury?" Jo's stomach clenched as she focused on that one word. "She hated the idea of you marrying me?"

"No, Jo. She was furious that she hadn't been present at the wedding. She's over the moon with joy that I married you." He shook his head and took a deep breath as he crossed his arms on his chest. "She's not going to be happy to hear the truth."

"She was *pleased?*"

"Why is that so hard to believe?"

"She doesn't know what happened?"

"She never knew we were seeing each other, no."

"I'm not talking about that," Jo snapped. "I know how well you kept that little secret."

Matt's eyes narrowed. "You mean does she know about the incident at work? Yes. She's a major shareholder, so of course she knows."

"And knowing that I'm accused of being a thief, she's still happy thinking we got married?"

"She doesn't think you're guilty."

"Hah! Everybody thinks I'm guilty."

Matt shook his head. "No. Not everybody. Just most people."

"Just most people?"

"Yeah. Including my father, who, unlike my mother, refuses to believe I'm a solid enough judge of character to be trusted when I say you didn't do it."

There was bitterness in his voice, which had her momentarily wondering if he could be telling the truth. He'd always *said* he believed her—but his actions hadn't borne it out. He'd cancelled the suspension, but nevertheless pushed her aside "while they investigate this," expected her to quietly stay out of the way in an obscure position on the other side of the city. In the eyes of her colleagues, that had clinched it—she had to be guilty.

"Careful, Matt, you might convince me you all along believed I was innocent," she retorted.

His mouth moved in what was half a grin, half a grimace. "I always did. I told you I did."

That was one way of putting it. He'd worked hard at hushing things up and hiding her away—and it had to be either because he believed she was guilty—or because he didn't want to embarrass himself if it came to light that he'd been involved with the person robbing the company.

After all, if he'd believed her—or if he had loved her, her brain inserted as a side note—he wouldn't have transferred her out of the main office, he wouldn't have gone along with having her office searched…. He would have come forward as the reason for her late nights at the office, those evenings when the computer logs showed that she hadn't touched her workstation.

She changed the subject. "None of this changes our current crisis—your mother is coming next month."

"I know. She's going to bring my grandmother, too."

He was being far too calm about this, while she could hear her own voice rising in an embarrassing approximation of hysteria. "Your mother and your grandmother are coming to meet me. Your *wife*."

"Yeah. I know."

She stared at him. "How can you be so calm about this?"

"I've had several hours to calm down. I even jogged almost five miles just to get rid of all that excess adrenaline."

Knowing that made her feel a little better, but maybe that was just because the image of Matt jogging did a great job of distracting her hormonal system. He was back in jeans and a shirt now. What had he worn while jogging?

Jo dragged her mind back to the matter at hand, trying to punch into her system that Matt's jogging attire didn't matter in the slightest.

"What are we going to do? Call her and tell her the truth?"

He shook his head, once. "If we don't want the truth to get out and possibly back to Esther, that wouldn't be a good idea. My mother isn't good with secrets."

Jo pulled out a kitchen chair and sat down abruptly.

"So what you suggest is that we let your mother think we're really married?"

"There's nothing else we can do at the moment, is there? But we have plenty of time. There are weeks until she plans to visit. Things may have changed by then. It's probably best just to play it by ear for a while."

"Did you talk to her?"

"I told you—she called. I wouldn't say we talked, exactly, but she talked *at* me, quite extensively."

"What do we do?" She buried her face in her hands. "Everything was in such a panic yesterday. We didn't think at all, did we?"

"We let Esther's gloomy talk draw us in."

"At least I did," Jo mumbled. "I was sure she was on her deathbed. For once, I should have listened to you. We can't keep this charade up forever. What can we do? Everybody will be expecting us to move in together."

"While Esther is sick—or pretending to be sick— it's understandable that we're staying with her."

"We?"

"I spent the day with Esther," he reminded her. "She's got strong opinions about the importance of married couples living together. If I go back to my apartment while you're staying here, she's going to suspect something's wrong. She really doesn't know we broke up, remember?"

"I don't care if she suspects something! She can't be expecting you to live here!"

"She can. She does. If you stay, as your husband, I stay. That's what she expects, like it or not. She expects us to want to be together the first days of our marriage—even under the circumstances."

Jo shook her head, almost speechless over the situation she was finding herself in. "She's probably lying and faking, and when she *expects* something—we just jump?"

"We already jumped, didn't we?" He shrugged. "The damage is done. We went this far, I don't think the situation can get much worse if we go along with this for a while longer."

"Don't be so sure. And despite appearances, there are limits to the rings I'm willing to run around that woman," Jo bit out. "She manipulated us. And now we have to stay in the same house together! It's horrible."

"Thank you," Matt drawled.

"I didn't mean you. Yes, I did mean you. Hell, I'm getting a headache," Jo groaned.

"You *are* a headache," Matt muttered. "And I think you work too hard at that new job. You look exhausted."

Jo barked a laugh. "I work too hard? That's rich, coming from Mr. Workaholic."

"I'm not a workaholic."

"Hah! You didn't even take the evening off on your birthday."

"Yes, I did."

Jo gritted her teeth and looked away. What in the world had possessed her to bring up his birthday? Matt had indeed taken the evening off, but that was because she'd sneaked into his office when everybody else had gone home and distracted him. The plan had been to take him out to dinner, but they'd never made it out of the building.

That day had been one of the incidents in evidence against her. The security cameras showed her entering the building after hours—but the logs showed she'd never turned on her own computer. The directors had demanded to know what she'd been doing. All she could do was stubbornly cling to her story of having done some paperwork in her office, say that she hadn't needed her computer, but it had been a weak argument. She hadn't thought she needed better arguments—she'd been sure Matt would explain when he got back from his trip, provide her with the alibi she needed.

He hadn't.

"Seriously, how long do we keep this up, Matt?"

Matt's shrug was noncommittal. "Until she's strong enough to take the truth, or until there is no longer need to pretend—or until we can find an easier lie to replace this one with. Any other ideas?"

"What do you mean, an easier lie?"

"We can divorce."

Jo stared at him. Then she laughed. This really was the icing on the cake. "This is fantastic, Matt. You mean, we get a fake divorce on top of everything else that's fake about this entire thing?"

Matt just shrugged.

"Well, that certainly is one solution. In the meantime, have you told your father yet that you married a spy and a thief?" she asked, not caring that bitterness was leaking off her tone.

Matt didn't flinch. "I don't believe you're a spy and a thief, Jo. I never did. Don't you even believe that much? What did I do to convince you of that?"

"You treated me like a spy and a thief."

"That's not true. I did what I had to do, the only thing I could do under the circumstances."

"Hide me away as if I was guilty and you were covering up for me?"

"I had the board to deal with, Jo. They'd already suspended you. I annulled the suspension, didn't I? All I did was transfer you for the time being, get you out of the way while we figured out what was going on. It was the only thing I could do—and it was difficult enough."

"You transferred me because you didn't believe me, you got me out of the way instead of going after the real culprit and proving my innocence."

Matt sighed, and this time the sigh got to her. He sounded tired, hopeless. Why? "We've had this conversation before, Jo. I had no choice. If I hadn't transferred you, there would have been some pretty dire consequences—not to mention a pretty hostile environment for you in the meantime. I went against the board's wishes, against my father's wishes—I did everything I could. Things could have gone a lot worse."

Worse than losing her job and the man she loved? She didn't think so.

She glanced at Matt, but looked away. It was discomfiting to see the weariness in his eyes.

"I did the best I could, Jo."

"Sure. Fine. Okay."

"Very convincing," he said dryly.

"There's no point in rehashing this. It's in the past."

"While you're still furious, it's not in the past."

"I'm over that."

"You're not."

"I have a new job. A job I got myself, without any help from you or anyone else. I'm happy. I'm doing

great. And I'll be doing even better when this ridiculous charade is over and I can go back to my normal
life.''

Matt stepped closer, invading her personal space
even though he didn't touch her. ''Let's have some
real honest emotion here, Jo, instead of this cold
shoulder.''

''Go away.''

''You never told me how angry you were at me,
Jo. You never yelled. You just told me in that icy
tone of yours that it was over and you never wanted
to see me again.''

''You were quick enough to take that for an answer.''

''You made yourself pretty clear when you said I'd
ruined your life.''

*If you'd loved me, you wouldn't have let that be
the end,* she wanted to say. But she didn't have the
right. ''You didn't believe me. You didn't trust me.''

''I was trying to protect you, Jo! It had nothing to
do with trust. It didn't matter if I believed you or not,
this could have ruined your career. I did the only
thing possible to salvage your reputation. It wasn't
easy for me either.''

''Am I supposed to be *grateful?*''

Matt shook his head in aggravation, but his eyes
were ablaze with emotion. ''You don't realize what
almost happened. Jo, if I hadn't stepped in, not only
could you have been fired, this would have gone to
the police. Did you realize how serious this was?''

''I was innocent!'' she spat back at him. ''If things
had gone to trial, I would have been acquitted.''

''I wanted to prove your innocence without going
through that. You know trials always color people,

even if they're innocent. You could have been branded forever.''

''And I'm not now?''

''No, you're not. Few people know about this at all.''

''Because you hushed things up, for the sake of the reputation of your precious company.''

He grabbed her wrist, but she yanked it away. ''For *your* sake, Jo.''

''It would never have gone to trial. There was no proof. There was circumstantial evidence at the best.''

''People are convicted on circumstantial evidence. There was no way of knowing what would have happened to you. They're coming down hard on white-collar crime these days, Jo. It isn't just punished by a slap on the wrist anymore.''

''The circumstantial evidence was planted. I didn't do it.'' She sank to the sofa and covered her eyes with her hands. ''Matt, you never even realized this was the worst part of it all, that you never believed me.''

''I believed you,'' he said in a low voice. ''That was never the issue. I never for a moment believed you were guilty.''

She looked up at him, again for a second wondering if that could be true. ''Why...''

''I had to do what I did, in order to get you—get *us*—out of this mess.''

''Transferring me away from my job? Getting me out of the company? Matt, you could as well have written Guilty on my forehead with a black marker. The few friends I had left were convinced of my guilt then.''

''The board had suspended you, Jo. I wasn't there, I had nothing to do with it.''

''Your *father* had suspended me.''

Matt sighed. ''We're talking in circles here. I cancelled the suspension and brought you back, remember?''

''Only to plant me in a distant corner of the galaxy instead.''

''You couldn't stay at the main office during the investigation, Jo. Don't you understand?''

''What investigation?'' She jumped away from him, trembling with anger now. ''There was to be no investigation. Your father made that clear. He just wanted to put this in the past, and I was an excellent scapegoat.''

''I know. He was wrong. You know I started an investigation as soon as I got back. It's still ongoing and we should have the results in soon. You'll be cleared. If you'd stayed, as I asked you to, you'd know all about it.''

Jo rubbed her face with her hands, feeling the exhaustion and anxiety of that time all over again. She couldn't have stayed in the job Matt had created for her so he could get her out of the office where she was considered a criminal—why didn't he understand that? ''Did your father ever find out about...us?''

Matt turned away now, crouching down by the cupboard where the dishwasher was to go and opening it. ''Yes. Where are we putting all this stuff?''

Her head snapped up. ''He did? How?''

''Today. Esther called everybody, remember?''

Suddenly her breathing seemed very loud in the silence. ''So? What was your father's response, finding out his new daughter-in-law is the 'immoral criminal' he had fired a few weeks ago?''

''Pretty predictable.''

''Angry?''

Matt piled up cans on the counter, gradually emptying the upper shelf. ''More like disgust.''

''Disgust?'' Jo frowned.

Matt looked up, impatiently tossing his head to get the hair out of his eyes. ''Don't you get it, Jo? Didn't you understand why I couldn't provide you with that alibi? Didn't you ever think about what would happen if I explained to people why you were at the office those evenings? Don't you realize how that would have looked?''

Realization came in a flash—and with it chagrin, almost horror, that she hadn't realized that sooner. She hadn't asked Matt to provide the alibi. She'd waited for him to offer it when he realized it was one of the big factors against her, and he hadn't, clinching her terrible suspicion that he was embarrassed about their relationship. ''Oh.''

Matt nodded. ''The company policy is clear, and it's strictly enforced. That's why we had to hide our relationship in the first place, remember? Providing you with an alibi would have made things worse, not better—it would have looked as though you'd been using me. So I did the only thing I could do—the best I could do for both of us. Got you out of there for the time being and started work on finding out the truth.'' He shoved both hands through his hair and turned away. ''Only it didn't quite work out the way I thought it would. You didn't cooperate.'' His groan echoed in the small kitchen. ''Do you have any idea how it looked when I fought so hard to get your suspension cancelled, and then you arrived the next morning with your box, emptied out your desk and vanished?''

Jo didn't know how to feel—what to think. Maybe she hadn't reacted rationally under the circumstances, but things had looked so black and white at the time. Anger—although she wasn't sure anymore if it was directed at him or herself—made her lash out at him again. ''Oh, that's just terrific. Now I'm supposed to thank you and apologize for not cooperating?''

''You never trusted me, Jo. I did everything in my power to protect you.''

''Protect me? I didn't need protection, I needed my name cleared.''

''To protect you *and* clear your name.''

''And you expected me to just take that job you planted me in?''

''Well—yes!''

''And keep seeing you.''

Matt squeezed his eyes shut in obvious frustration. ''This had nothing to do with you and me. Nothing! It was just business.''

''Just business,'' she repeated, her voice almost a whisper now. ''And it ruined everything, didn't it?''

Matt wasn't looking at her. He was staring out the window, his profile hard now. ''We allowed it to ruin everything, Jo. It was our own fault.''

After dinner, the three of them spent the evening in front of the television, Jo and Esther watching a movie, Matt on a recliner with his laptop, still working, his face serious in the pale glow from the screen. She couldn't help herself—her gaze strayed constantly from the antics of the actors on the television screen and to the face of the man who for a short while, such a short time ago, had been the most important being in the world to her.

It was hard, straddling that fence between intimate lovers and casual pseudo-relatives. Hard to know how to treat him. Painful just to look at him.

He glanced up and met her gaze, raising an eyebrow in question. She gestured at his computer. "You're still working on the Ottesen project?" she asked.

He looked at her, startled, almost as if he'd forgotten she'd once been a vital part of that project. "Yes. We'll be working on it until the end of summer, probably."

"What did you decide?" Curiosity pushed her forward, trying to sneak a look at Matt's screen. This had been in part her project, many of her ideas were mingled in the data and blueprints on Matt's screen.

Matt glanced up at her, and despite their conversation, despite the blinders that had been ripped from her eyes, the remains of her former convictions inched toward the forefront of her mind. He might still think she was an industrial spy. Of course he wouldn't want to show her his work, she might sell it to the highest bidder.

Matt shook his head, evidently reading her mind without effort. "No, Jo," he said in a low voice so Esther wouldn't hear. "Do you still not believe me? How long are you going to keep this up? I'm not afraid to show you my work."

"It's fine," she said. "I'm not that interested."

Matt dumped the laptop on her knees and stood, walking toward the kitchen. "I'm going to get something to drink. Look as much as you like. Can I get you something, Esther? Or you, Jo?''

Jo shook her head, and watched him head toward the kitchen, realizing he didn't like being close to her any more than she did to him. Pushing the thought away, she adjusted the screen and started looking through the contents of the file. A lot had happened in the last month. Some of the changes she agreed with, others not. It was only to be expected.

Matt returned, carrying ice tea for Esther and a beer for himself. Jo handed him back the laptop. ''Thanks for letting me take a look.''

''No problem,'' he said. ''What do you think?''

Jo hesitated, then launched into an explanation of what she did and didn't like. Matt listened attentively, taking the occasional note, and she almost forgot their past. This was what it had been like in the beginning, after she'd started working for him, and before they'd become lovers. She'd excitedly told him her ideas, her proposals, and he'd listened, sometimes pointing out problems from his own vastly superior experience, sometimes asking questions that reduced her plans to ashes, but most of the time guiding her forward until her ideas become something more, something better. He was an excellent teacher. It was one of the things she'd liked best about working with him.

Esther went early to bed, planning to finish a book on tape, and Jo used the opportunity to escape to her room as well.

''Night,'' she told him, then paused. ''Did you solve the mystery of the missing sheets today?''

''Not sure,'' Matt said dryly. ''Apparently one of the bridge ladies borrowed them, but I didn't quite follow her explanation of why.''

"What are you going to do?"

"I guess I'll take the blanket. I should have gone home and fetched my own sheets today."

"You still can. Or, if you'd rather, you can try to get that sleeping bag from the attic. I found a flashlight this morning, it's on the kitchen counter."

Why did she care? Why was she helping?

Matt glanced up, his eyes focusing on hers again. There was warmth in them again—or was it a trick of the lighting? "Sleeping bag—attic. Flashlight—kitchen. Okay. Thanks."

"Are you going to work tomorrow?"

He nodded. "Esther seems fine. She has plans of having friends over. I'll try to get back early though, see that she eats properly."

"How are we…" She paused. The plan had been to play it by ear for a few days. It wouldn't do any good to agonize over the details. "Never mind. Good night."

"Night, Jo."

CHAPTER FIVE

WHEN Joanna arrived home, Matt wasn't there yet, but Grandma was standing in the hallway, hands on hips, and looking like a stooped, gray-haired Fury.

"You're not sleeping together!"

Grandma balanced anger, upset and hurt nicely, with a healthy dose of completely unjustifiable indignation thrown in. Jo fought the urge to tell her to mind her own business, then succumbed. It was only the honest truth, and the old lady seemed sturdy enough to take it. "Our sleeping arrangements really aren't any of your business, Grandma."

"Why are you sleeping in separate bedrooms? Didn't you even spend your wedding night together? What sort of a marriage is it that starts off in separate beds?"

Jo put her briefcase down and removed her coat. "Grandma, I love you to pieces—but I repeat: this is none of your business, so put it out of your mind. Did you go upstairs? By yourself? Where's Matt?"

"Matt went to the grocery store. I may or may not be dying, but I'm not an invalid. I needed something from my bedroom upstairs. And guess what I saw. A sleeping bag on my bed. A sleeping bag! What do you think this is, a camping site?"

"Well, all the sheets were gone, so a sleeping bag was the only option until we can find them. Any idea where they might be, Grandma?"

"A friend borrowed them for a few days. She'll be

93

returning everything before the weekend. But that's neither here nor there. We're talking about your marriage now. You're married! You should sleep in the same room!''

"Your record is broken, Grandma," Jo told her, softening the words with a kiss on her cheek. She heard the front door open and shut, and then felt Matt's presence behind her. Grandma found a new victim to fix with her icy stare. "You're not sleeping together! Why?''

The question didn't seem to surprise him. "That isn't any of your business, Esther," Matt said calmly. "It's between me and Jo, and whether we sleep in the same room is our decision. Plenty of couples have separate beds, even separate bedrooms. Butt out—and I mean that nicely." Just as Jo had, he kissed Esther's cheek in compensation for his harsh words.

Esther glowered at him, then turned an accusing eye back on Jo. Despite deep admiration for Matt's "butt out" philosophy she did not feel up to sending her grandmother quite such an explicit message herself.

"You don't know the damage this can do to your marriage," the old lady said darkly. "This is no way to start a marriage."

"Grandma, it's not a big deal. We're just not… I mean…" Jo looked at Matt, pleading for help. He shrugged. "Grandma, Matt snores," she explained, proud of her sudden inspiration, although the barb of Matt's stare practically stabbed her temple. He didn't snore, and she knew that very well. "The noise is terrible," she continued, warming to her subject. "It's like trying to sleep in a noisy factory. I do need my sleep if I am to function at all at work.''

"Talk to a doctor," Grandma said promptly, but Jo thought she saw relief in her eyes at this simple explanation. "Snoring can be fixed. I saw something about it on TV. And if it can't be fixed, in the meantime there are always earplugs. In my experience, a sharp jab with an elbow also does the trick. Whatever works. Nothing is worse for a marriage than separate beds. Take my word for it."

Matt grinned at Grandma. "I'll talk to a doctor, Esther."

"Good. And Jo, you will buy earplugs today?"

Jo rolled her eyes. "Grandma…"

"I'm sure Matt will have the snoring under control soon, but in the meantime, earplugs work wonders. I should know, your grandfather snored something terrible the last ten years of his life, bless him. Come to think of it, there might even be a small stash of earplugs left over, somewhere around here."

"I don't like to wear earplugs, Grandma, even antique ones. We'll wait for the doctor's verdict, and in the meantime Matt will borrow your room."

Esther pretended not to hear. "Well, it doesn't matter. The point is moot anyway, as I'll be moving up to my bedroom now."

Jo narrowed her eyes and folded her arms on her chest, suspicion radiating off her. "I see. You're feeling that much better that you can handle the stairs again?"

"Absolutely. The stairs are good exercise for me. And I look forward to sleeping in my own bed."

"Fine." Matt patted Jo on the shoulder. "But don't worry, darling, you won't have to put up with my snoring. I'll sleep downstairs in the guest room, then."

Grandma looked chagrined at this small hitch in her rather obvious plan. Then she looked cunning for a microsecond, before shaking her head. She whistled for Aron and Aaron, and the dogs rushed to her side. She ushered them toward the front door.

"Grandma!" Jo rushed after Esther. "What are you doing?"

"I'm going to walk the dogs."

"Walk the dogs? Outside? By yourself?"

"Yes. It'll do me good. You know I like to go for a daily walk."

"You're going for a *walk?*" Matt asked. "You feel up to taking a walk?"

"Yes. I'm feeling much better." She smiled, even as Jo and Matt looked at each other, dumbfounded. "Maybe I'll even live to see your children. That would be nice. Not that I'm pushing or anything. I understand that a couple may want time to themselves before that. Besides," she muttered under her breath as she grabbed her coat, smile replaced with a petulant frown. "There's not much chance of you having children while you're sleeping in separate rooms, is there?"

Jo suppressed a snarl. Matt helped Esther with her coat. "I'll join you," he said. "I don't get nearly enough exercise, anyway."

"You're lying, Matt," Esther murmured, pulling on her gloves and searching the shelves for her umbrella. "It's obvious even to me that you're in great shape. But it's nice of you to accompany an old lady."

"Be careful," Jo called after them, standing in the front door. "Just a short walk. You've hardly been out of bed for more than two weeks, don't overdo it."

She stared after the two of them. Grandma had her cane, but she wasn't even leaning on it, and only had a light hold on Matt's arm. And she was *striding*. Matt didn't even have to adjust his steps to hers.

Jo stared after them until they disappeared. There was no question about it: Grandma was back to her normal, robust, healthy self. Which of course, left the dilemma: how to get out of this "marriage" to Matt that everybody now knew about.

But at least Grandma's little bedroom scheme wouldn't work—she might be moving up to her own room, but there was still the downstairs guest room for Matt to sleep in. Jo grinned as she turned toward the guest room, hoping there would be some extra sheets in the closets there.

Grandma might be forcing them to live together, but she wouldn't win this battle.

After dinner, the three of them had settled down to a game of Scrabble in the living room when the doorbell chimed. Esther jumped to her feet with all the energy of a fifteen-year-old and almost ran to the door. Jo and Matt looked at each other, sensing trouble ahead.

There was noise out front. Matt closed his eyes and groaned. "What now?"

They stared at each other, a strange truce in the air now that they were both aware of the trap they were in. "Do we want to know?" Jo asked, eyeing the doorway. "Should we go check, do you think?"

Matt slowly shrugged, cocking his head to the side to listen. She did the same. There was a murmur of voices. There was some kind of squeaking noise. The dogs went crazy, but were quickly hushed. Then there were whispers and strange noises, and movement at the front of the house. Jo braced her elbows on the table, rested her head on her hands and closed her eyes. "I don't think I want to know."

"I agree. I suppose we could just wait and hope for the best."

"Yeah, let's do that." She started to rearrange the tiles on her slate. "I'll try to get a triple word score while Grandma is away. She never gives me enough time to think."

Matt chuckled. "If everybody took the time you take, each game would last a week."

His tone was indulgent, and when she glanced up there was a faraway smile on his face. Something inside tightened as she realized he was remembering their own Scrabble games. She looked back down at her letters and concentrated.

Esther finally got rid of her company and came back, but that did not leave the house silent.

"What *is* that noise?" Jo asked, still not sure she wanted to know, and the way Matt was huddled over his own tiles told her he wasn't any keener to find out just what the old lady and her buddies were up to this time.

Esther maneuvered back into her seat and fiddled with her letters. "Oh, nothing. Just a few birds I'll be baby-sitting for a couple of days. Nothing for you to worry about."

"*Birds?*" Jo yelled.

"Birds?" Matt repeated. He leaned back in his chair and rubbed his forehead with a hand, looking almost resigned. "I see. Birds. Inside the house?"

"Yes. Parrots. The big kind. Very colorful and beautiful. They don't speak though. Not English, anyway. Don't think it's French either. Maybe it's Spanish—don't they all come from South America originally? Or is it Africa? Anyway, whichever language it is, they do squeak quite a bit, don't they?''

''The sound is coming from the guest room.'' Jo jumped out of her seat to follow Matt as he strode out of the room and toward the guest room. He opened the door, and from a few steps behind, Jo saw his jaw drop. ''Esther...'' he groaned. ''What have you done?''

Jo stopped. He was blocking the doorway, and she didn't want to get too close to him. It tended to make her shiver. ''What? What's in there?''

Matt looked toward her and gestured. ''Look for yourself.''

Jo carefully inched closer in the narrow space Matt left between himself and the doorjamb. Her mouth fell open in astonishment equal to Matt's as she saw inside.

''Oh, my God,'' she said in a high squeaky tone.

In the half hour she'd used to compose the word *irrupt* for a double word score, the guest room had been demolished. The furniture had been squeezed into corners, and draped in plastic. In the middle of the room there was a huge cage, reaching almost from floor to ceiling.

Inside were six colorful birds.

''She's doing this to make you sleep in my room,'' Jo said, her voice on the verge of hysteria. ''She's turned the guest room into a zoo just to force us to sleep together. Can you believe it?''

''Yes.'' Matt was actually chuckling. Then he rested his head against the wall and closed his eyes and the chuckles turned into full-blown laughter, although he kept it quiet enough not to reach Esther's ears.

Jo looked into the guest-room-turned-aviary. ''Get a grip, Matt. This isn't funny. We're not going to let her get away with this, are we?''

''It *is* funny. It's hilarious.''

''Well, turn off your sense of humor!'' Jo hissed. ''This is serious. We're pretending to be married, remember? We're pretending to be in love! Well, I don't want to do it forever, so we have to do something about this!''

Matt's grin died, and as they stepped out of the door, he pulled the door shut, dampening the noise of the birds. ''Do something about this? Of course.''

He turned around and strode back to the lounge where Esther was sitting, innocently playing with her Scrabble tiles. He sat opposite the old lady, and leaned on his elbows toward her. ''Esther...there are six huge parrots in the guest room.''

''I know, dear,'' Esther said without even looking up from her tiles. ''Nora's grandson raises them. They'll be staying with us for just a little while. They're no problem, just keep the door shut and the noise shouldn't bother you too much.''

''This is ridiculous...'' Jo sputtered.

Esther gestured vaguely. ''They needed a place for them, just for a while.''

''How long is a while?''

''I don't know, a week, a month, however long it takes.''

''However long what takes?'' Jo asked.

Grandma finally peered up at her over her glasses. ''Is there a problem, dear?''

Is there a problem, dear? Had she seriously asked that?

"Yes. Yes, Grandmother, there is a problem. Matt was going to sleep in there, you know that."

"Matt should sleep in your bed, anyway. Did you buy earplugs yet?"

Jo went back to other arguments—Grandma loved her house. "There are six birds! The noise, the smell...we'll never get the smell out of that room!"

"Nonsense. Nora promised to take care of all that. The room will be good as new. There are no carpets there, which minimizes the smell problem, and we took out the loose rugs. We should probably take down the drapes too, shouldn't we?"

"The noise!"

"They're downstairs, dear. Won't bother us at all. And, well, you'll be wearing earplugs anyway, won't you, because of Matt's snoring?"

"You're doing this to make us sleep in the same room. Well, it won't work. I won't be forced to sleep with...to stay awake all night just because you think a wife should learn to tolerate her husband's snoring. I have a job to go to in the morning and I need my sleep."

Esther waved a hand at her, and frowned down at her Scrabble slate. "Ssshhh, dear, I'm trying to concentrate here. I only have one vowel and some tricky consonants."

Jo turned on her heel and stalked into the kitchen for a reprieve. She couldn't remember ever having been tempted to yell at her grandmother before, but she sure was now.

Matt had followed her. She twisted around, gesturing randomly in her wrath. "Can you believe this?"

"She's one determined lady," he acknowledged, the small grin on his face totally infuriating.

She glared at him. "You still find this funny, don't you?"

"Yes. Don't you?"

Jo shook her head. "No. No, I don't. Maybe in ten years time I'll see this as brilliant comedy, but not now. This isn't working out. We have to tell her right now, end this charade."

"Are you sure? She may have manipulated us into marriage, but are you sure you want to tell her not only is this a pretend marriage, but we're not even together anymore? You know it's going to break her heart."

"Oh, hell." Jo's anger drained out of her in an instant. "No, Matt, of course I don't want to tell her. That's why we got into this mess in the first place, remember? Because I didn't tell her! I just couldn't. Even if she's not sick, she's still old and frail and she was so happy that we were together...but we have to tell her somehow, sometime..."

"She's a devious manipulator, but she's a devious manipulator that we love. I'm sure we'll figure something out soon—as soon as she admits she's back to normal. I'll just sleep on the sofa tonight."

"Or you could go home," Jo suggested hopefully. "Why not? This is just a temporary situation anyway, with me staying here. It's perfectly understandable that you sleep at your place until..."

"Until we move in together?" Matt supplied when she ran out of steam.

"Very funny."

"I haven't seen you smile for weeks. Did I ruin

your sense of humor along with your career and your life?''

His voice was dry, and she had a feeling he was quoting her. She might have said something along those lines. Yes, she had accused him of ruining her life and her career. At the time, it had felt like the truth—because his denial of their relationship had left her heart in pieces.

''No. My sense of humor is fine. There just hasn't been much to smile about recently.''

''I could tell you a joke.''

Jo groaned, but the simple mention of Matt telling a joke had a smile jerk at her lips. She couldn't help it. ''No. Please don't tell me a joke. You're the worst joke-teller in the world.''

''It always makes you laugh.''

''Yes, but I laugh *at* you, not with you. You're worse than a four-year-old. Your jokes are so unfunny that it's hysterical. It's not fair. Please don't tell me a joke.''

Matt grinned. ''Okay. Let's finish the game and put our torturer to bed.''

''Well, I'm going to bed,'' Jo announced, giving in before Esther did. She had a job to go to in the morning—Esther didn't. Matt, on the other hand, did, and he noticed Jo send him a pitying glance. He hoped he'd get Esther to vacate the sofa soon. It was the only remaining sleeping space in the house. ''Good night,'' Jo chirped before vanishing up the stairs.

''Night,'' Esther and Matt echoed. Then Esther sent her godson a glare. ''Aren't you going with her? You'll have to stay in her room, snores or not. I'll be using my room, and the guest room is occupied.''

"Jo needs to get to work in the morning. I'm not going to keep her up with my snoring, so I'm sleeping right here on this sofa, Esther."

His voice was firm and determined, but it didn't seem to make the slightest difference to Esther. She just got more comfortable in her corner of the sofa, smugly clutching the remote control. "You can't sleep while I'm watching TV, can you?"

"No problem. I'll stay awhile longer, and watch TV with you."

"You're newlyweds. Go tuck your wife in, Matthew. I'll be fine. I intend to stay up awhile."

"I'll wait."

A few hours later, at 3:00 a.m., Grandma was making a fresh batch of popcorn in preparation for a documentary about flower pressing.

And Matt was exhausted.

He rubbed the face of his watch, confirming how late it was, and tried to stifle a yawn. Time had passed slowly the last couple of hours.

Wouldn't she *ever* go to bed? There was no way he was going to get any sleep, not sitting up and with the TV on.

"Why don't you go to bed, Matthew?" Esther suggested, trotting back with her bowl of popcorn. "You have to get up at six. It's nice of you to want to keep me company, but you should go to bed."

"What about you?" he protested. "Shouldn't you get to bed?"

"Insomnia is one of the side effects of old age," Esther informed him as she sat down and pulled the blanket over her legs. "I just need a couple of hours these days."

"So you're not going to bed any time soon?" he asked, resigned.

"Television is such a wonderful invention, isn't it?"

Devious lady. Matt gave up. He stood up, kissed Esther on the cheek and bade her good night before heading upstairs.

If Esther was going to be sleeping down here, fine, he'd steal her bed. Why hadn't that occurred to him before? He smiled in triumph as he reached her door.

But life was never that easy. Anticipating his move, Esther had actually resorted to locking her bedroom door.

Obviously, this was war.

Matt leaned back against Esther's bedroom door and groaned, staring at Jo's door on the opposite wall. What he wouldn't do for a couple of hours of sleep. It wasn't as if he'd gotten any decent sleep for the last two nights.

Jo's bed *was* plenty big enough for both of them. And he needed to get up in three hours. She wouldn't begrudge him a quarter of the mattress for a couple of hours, would she?

He knocked softly on the door, then harder when there was no response. Jo had always been a sound sleeper. He tried the doorknob. It was unlocked, and he tiptoed inside, not sure what he was going to do. Just crawl into bed beside her, hoping she wouldn't even notice he was there until morning? Wake her up and ask for permission?

He'd never get her permission if he asked.

The dilemma was solved as Jo sat up in bed, gasping like an insulted virgin sacrifice. "Matt? What the hell are you doing in here?"

Her outrage somehow made it easy for him to make up his mind. He ignored her shocked gasp and started undressing. He had work tomorrow, meetings and important engagements. She'd gotten hours of sleep, he deserved a few winks too. It wasn't as if they hadn't shared a bed before. "It's past three in the morning and your grandmother is still downstairs, watching TV. And she locked her door, so I can't even steal her bed."

"I don't care. You can't sleep here."

"Be reasonable, Jo." He raked a hand through his hair and hoped he looked pitiful. "Hell, be merciful. I can't sleep anywhere else. Your grandmother's room is locked, the living room is occupied, and the guest room has been turned into a bird conservatory."

"Why don't you just go home?" Jo was peering at him in the darkness and he remembered her myopia. She was practically blind without her contacts, and it was one of the cutest things in the world to watch her fumble for her glasses in the morning. "We can't let her get away with this!" she hissed. "This is exactly what she wants! Don't you see? You're playing right into her hands!"

"I know." He kept undressing. "But I'm not driving home now, it's a two-hour drive and by the time I got home, it would be time to get up."

"I don't care. You're not sleeping in my bed."

"Give me one good reason why."

Only one? Jo was feeling disoriented, having woken up so suddenly. She knew there were a million reasons, but it was difficult to articulate them at this precise moment. "Because I don't want you to," she ended up saying.

"Jo!" Matt was looking grim, as well as exhausted. He was also looking rather...naked by now. She could see that even without her contacts. "I don't care what you do. You can put a coil of barbed wire in the middle of the bed, a nest of cobras, an execution squad. You can even put Esther there. I don't care. I'm not going to touch you. I just need to *sleep.*"

He ripped the covers off the unoccupied side of the bed and got in. "Good night."

"Okay," she said. There wasn't a choice. She couldn't exactly pick him up and cart him out. At least in the bed he'd be decently covered up and her insides might stop trembling. "But stay on your side of the bed."

"Absolutely. Wouldn't dream of anything else," Matt muttered into his pillow, and she turned on her side, resolutely facing the other direction. The bed was big enough. What was she worried about?

Well, she might be worrying about her old habit of rolling close to Matt, putting her arm around him and her leg around one of his, ensuring that he wasn't going anywhere. She might be worrying about his old habit of kissing her in his sleep whenever he moved. Then there was the slight problem of the way they'd always woken up tangled in a heap that, to their mutual pleasure, had always taken a while to untangle.

Dammit. She'd never get to sleep now.

She sat up. "Matt?"

"Yes?" His voice sounded drowsy. He wasn't seriously falling asleep? With no trouble at all? How infuriating!

How *rude!*

"I really don't think we should be doing this. I mean it. It'll only encourage Grandma, and we're in big enough trouble already, don't you think? This is exactly what she wants us to do.''

Matt was silent for a couple of seconds and she was wondering if he'd fallen asleep when he spoke again. ''Not quite. She'd not approve of us clinging to the edges of the bed like this and leaving a wasteland in the middle.''

''You know what I mean.''

''I don't care. I have a lot of work to catch up on tomorrow, and I could really use some sleep.''

There was silence for a while, until she could hear his breathing even out. He was going to fall asleep in a matter of minutes, right there next to her! How could he do that?

''How long do you suppose we keep this up?'' she asked in a loud voice.

''Don't know,'' Matt murmured. He sounded like he didn't much care at the moment. Well, he was not getting away with just falling asleep.

''We can't do this much longer. We'll have to tell her the truth.''

''What's the truth?''

She turned to face him, but his back was still to her. This had sounded suspiciously like a rhetorical question. He wasn't talking in his sleep, was he? ''You know, Matt. The closest we can get to the truth. We need to tell her that we're not in love and don't want to be married. That it was a mistake, we realize we're not meant to be together.''

''I see.''

''We don't have a choice, Matt, we have to tell her. She's doing fine; I hope she'll live for many more years. I'm not prepared to go through this farce for years, and I'm sure you're no more eager than I am.

She's going to expect me to move in with you, or us to buy a house together—I'm not going to take this lie that far. We'd never get away with it, anyway.''

"What do you suggest?''

"I don't know!''

"That's why I suggest waiting and seeing. If you don't have a better suggestion…?''

"How long?''

"I don't know. That's the 'wait and see' part.''

"I can't do this,'' Jo said. She shook her head, not that he'd see it, turned away from her in the darkness. "I can't keep this up. It exhausts me to pretend like this—and your mother hasn't even shown up yet.''

"You *can't* keep this up? You mean you don't want to.''

"Does it make a difference?''

"We've come this far. Trust me, to keep going will be easier than backtracking now.''

"Trust you?" Jo squeezed the sheet at her chest, furious now. "Remember the last time you asked me to trust you?''

Matt's frustrated sigh was almost a growl. "I have to be at work in a couple of hours—I don't feel up to defending myself again. Would you *please* let me get some sleep before we go back to the ongoing grand trial?''

Jo stood up and grabbed her robe. "Night.''

Matt sat up. "Where are you going?''

"Downstairs to watch TV with Grandma.''

CHAPTER SIX

MATT didn't sleep at all for the rest of the night, and Jo never came back to bed. When he went downstairs early in the morning, he found her on the sofa, dark circles under her eyes, and her head resting on an embroidered cushion. A blanket was draped over her, and he fought the urge to tuck her in closer. He touched her hair with the tips of her fingers. Short bristles, still.

It *would* grow back. Somehow that had become his mantra these days.

Esther was standing in the door when he straightened up, a frown darkening her face. She beckoned for him to come to her, and he did so, sighing.

"Why is Jo sleeping on the sofa?" she demanded. Matt patted her shoulder.

"Butt out, Esther."

"That's disrespectful."

"So is interrogating us about our personal life."

"It's just not right, Matthew!"

He kissed her on the cheek. "Jo needs to wake up in twenty minutes, for work. Will you wake her? She doesn't have an alarm clock down here and I know she hates being late for work."

"I'll wake her," Esther said grudgingly. "I'll give her a piece of my mind too."

"No!" He pulled Esther with him to the kitchen and pointed to a chair. "Sit down, Esther."

She did, rather to his surprise. He put his hands on

his hips and loomed over her, hoping to intimidate the old lady for once. "Don't interrogate Jo. Don't push her. This is not your problem. Leave us to handle it."

"You *are* having problems, aren't you? And don't give me that nonsense about snoring. I know Jo wouldn't let that keep her away from you at night."

"If we are, they are our problems. Not yours."

"There are professionals who can help with such issues," Esther said, fiddling with the sash on her robe. "I know I pushed you into marriage. If there is a problem, I feel responsible. There must be something we can do about it. Isn't there?"

"Don't worry about this. Just leave us to it. It's our marriage now—despite your fingers in it, and yes, you shouldn't have pushed us, but it's over and done with now. You're not our marriage counselor, okay?"

Esther nodded. "I won't talk to Jo about why she's on the sofa," she said with a sigh. "But I really should have a talk with you about why *she's* the one on the sofa. That's not gentlemanly."

"I've got to go, Esther," he told her, glad to have a good reason to escape. "Save your gentleman lecture until later, okay?"

Esther scowled at him. "Fine. But don't think you're off the hook."

"Never," he assured her, and headed for the front door. Jo was still on the sofa, sound asleep as he passed her.

No, he wasn't off the hook.

The investigation was finally over. Jo's name had been cleared.

Matt gnawed on a pencil and stared at the investigative report. It was thorough, detailed, and left no room for doubt. There was even a warning that she'd have excellent grounds to sue and a recommendation that the company settle with her quietly and peacefully if that was in any way possible.

He should be worried about the risk of her suing the company. He should also be furious over his betrayal by one of the people he'd trusted—a man who'd been with the firm for almost a decade, who not only had betrayed his trust, but had picked Jo to frame for his crimes.

But his mind wasn't on the job at hand.

Instead all he did was obsess about how to turn this pretend relationship of theirs back into a real one.

He shook his head in attempt to rid it of old memories and concentrated on the open report on his desk. How had things gone so out of hand in the first place? How had Jo gotten in such deep trouble with such flimsy evidence?

So many factors had combined. He'd been away and his father had been determined to close the matter with a minimum of fuss. Jo's furious departure from the company after he'd come back and tried to reinstate her hadn't helped the issue. By the time the dust had settled, everybody was convinced she must be guilty.

Well, now they would know differently.

He reached for the phone, intending to call Jo with the good news, but slowly withdrew his hand. She would be vindicated—but there was their relationship to consider.

He rested his head in his hands and tried to think. If he started with the news that her name had been cleared, she'd think he'd only wanted her back when the investigators had proven her innocence.

When the phone rang, and Jo's voice came over the line, nervous and stubborn as ever, his determination doubled. They had unfinished business—and if postponing this a few days would help, then he would.

"I'm telling her the truth tonight," Jo said, her voice just this side of trembling.

Matt balanced the phone on his shoulder and started up his e-mail program. First things first—he'd let everybody at the company know Jo was innocent. He grinned as he remembered the special frown Jo used to give him if he kept working while they talked—it had always driven her crazy. "Are you sure that's smart?"

"No. But we have no choice. I can't go on like this, and it's not fair to any of us."

"What do we tell people?"

"I don't care."

Matt sent off his e-mail and leaned back in his chair, feeling better already. Everybody who'd doubted Jo would know the truth now. Next issue: his personal battle strategy.

"I see. We'll discuss it, okay? I'll pick you up around five, and we'll decide on the way home when and how to tell her. Okay?"

"Fine," Jo said grudgingly.

Despite the long drive, they were still far from having resolved the issue of whether or not to tell Esther the truth, when they got home to find a visitor in the living room with her.

Esther cheerfully summoned them, introducing the

man with a sweeping hand wave. Matt noticed that his hair was almost as long as Jo's used to be. "This is Dr. Walters."

Matt shook hands with the doctor, while Jo rushed to her grandmother. "What's wrong, Grandma?"

"I'm fine," Esther beamed. "Just fine."

"Why did you call the doctor? And why not Dr. Harrier like you always do? What's wrong?"

"Dr. Walters is for you two," Esther said sweetly, before grabbing her cane and hoisting herself to her feet. "He's a therapist."

There was total silence in the room for a few moments, broken only by the sound of Esther's cane against the rug as she made her way toward the door.

"You hired a therapist for us?" Jo asked weakly. "Grandma..."

"Yes, love. I hope he can help you." Esther hurried from the room and closed the door quietly behind her, leaving Jo and Matt to stare at each other, and then at the therapist standing in front of them.

Now what?

"Why don't we have a seat?" the doctor said cheerfully, looking just as much at home as if he were in his own office. He sat down, crossed his legs and looked at them patiently. Matt shrugged and sank down on the sofa, beckoning Jo to follow. "I can't believe this," he muttered. "You're a marriage counselor?"

"Something like that," the man confirmed. "I specialize in helping couples who are having problems with marital relations."

"Marital relations...?" His worst suspicions bobbed to the surface. Esther couldn't have... No, she couldn't possibly have... He glanced at Jo and saw an answering expression of rising horror, so it wasn't just his paranoia speaking. It really was... "You don't mean...?"

"I specialize in sexual problems," Dr. Walters confirmed with a modest smile.

Matt watched Jo lean forward in slow motion until her forehead met her knees. "Oh, God," he heard her mumble. "Grandma hired us a sex therapist."

Matt cleared his throat. "Dr. Walters...this is a misunderstanding. We aren't having any problems. We have no need for a...therapist. Any kind of therapist." He looked to Jo for confirmation, but her face was hidden. "We're doing fine."

The doctor responded to that by getting a pad and a pen out of his briefcase. "Yes, Mrs. Brande told me that would probably be your response. She is very concerned for you. She tells me you two haven't been sharing a bedroom, not even on your wedding night. It is a natural conclusion that you are facing some unexpected problems in the marriage bed."

Jo's head was still pressed to her knees, leaving him alone to deal with the therapist. He clenched his teeth in the effort to be civil. "Mrs. Brande means well," he said. "But this is a misunderstanding. We're not having any problems. She called you here for nothing."

The doctor made a note on his pad. Why? What note was that? What had he said that warranted a note?

The doctor looked up at him over his glasses. "It's nothing to be ashamed of, Matthew—may I call you Matthew? This isn't an uncommon problem."

"What problem? We're not having any problems!"

"Many men have problems with performance anxiety as newlyweds—"

"I do not have performance anxiety!" Matt exploded, straining to keep himself from hyperventilating. Where had Esther found this guy? *Why* had Esther found this guy? What had Jo been telling her?

Jo's shoulders were shaking. He wasn't sure if she was laughing or just hiding in embarrassment. He hoped she wasn't laughing. She'd *better* not be laughing at his "performance anxiety."

"You don't think it's performance anxiety." Dr. Walters nodded, concern on his face. "I see. Is it a question of...endurance perhaps? That's a common—"

"I have plenty of endurance!" Matt yelled.

"There's no need to be embarrassed, Matthew. Plenty of men have problems with—"

"I do *not* have a *problem!*"

Dr. Walters wisely closed his mouth, but was quick to recover. He made another note on his pad. Matt squinted, but couldn't make it out.

"I see. Matthew, you do not think you have any problems. I want to ask you to keep in mind anyway that the first step toward solving a problem is acknowledging the possibility of its existence." He wisely switched subjects before Matt could comment. "Now, let's continue. Is it Joanna, perhaps, who's having problems? It's not an uncommon problem that the husband isn't aware of some of the subtleties in his wife's anatomy..."

"I know all I need to know about my wife's..." Matt broke off and swore, clenching his fists. He had to stop shouting. Esther, upstairs, didn't need to know about his in-depth knowledge of Jo's anatomy. "So

even if *she's* the one having problems, it's *my* fault, is it?''

Another note was scribbled. As the doctor leaned toward him, Matt finally got a look at his clipboard. "Husb. defens." it said. "There is no need to establish guilt or responsibility," Dr. Walters said in a voice that was probably supposed to be calming, but that did an excellent job of driving his blood pressure even further up. "Guilt serves no purpose in this matter. But what you may have here is a breakdown in communications. If there is a problem, it may be because one of you isn't giving the other one some needed information or feedback. That's something that can easily be resolved through some open and honest discussion. That's what we're here for.''

Matt whimpered. It was all he could do, but now Jo had at least raised herself up. She was still covering her face with her hands, and what little he could see was redder than the rose petals that had littered her bed on their wedding night. He narrowed his eyes, pried two of her fingers away for a confirmation of what he was seeing, and then leaned toward the doctor with a smile. "Actually, you're right," he confided in the man. "Joanna is having some problems, but it's not a communications problem. She's been very explicit in telling me what she wants, when, where and how.''

He heard Joanna gasp in horror and she removed one hand from her face and made an attempt at pinching his thigh, but he grabbed her hand and held it tightly in the gesture of the loving husband. He'd managed to see the truth when he'd pulled her fingers away from her face.

She *was* laughing—so hard she had tears streaming

from her eyes, and despite everything her laughter loosened something around his heart, something he hadn't even realized had been frozen. He felt his own face start to relax into laughter—but the issue remained. His masculinity was in question now.

Well, they'd just see who had the last laugh. "To be honest, doctor, it's her…special requests that are a bit of a problem."

"I see." The doctor turned to Joanna, beaming with pleasure at this breakthrough. "We've narrowed the issue down. Good. Excellent progress. Tell me about your problem, Joanna."

"Matt…" Jo begged. "Please. Save us."

Matt put his arm over Jo's shoulders, his other hand resting on top of hers in her lap. "This isn't easy for her. My wife is a little embarrassed about her problem."

"Matt!"

Matt tightened his arm around her and shook her a bit. "Tell the doctor, darling. We have to be open and honest about this."

Jo's voice lowered and she snatched her hand out of his, pulling away from him and perching on the edge of the sofa. "You're a dead man, Matt…"

Matt cleared his throat and grabbed Jo's hands back in his own. "Okay, darling, I'll tell him. You see, she has these fantasies that she likes to act out…"

Dr. Walters leaned forward, hanging on every word, while Jo tore her hands free and covered her face again. "Yes?" the doctor prompted. "And those fantasies?"

Matt nudged Jo. "Darling? You can do it. Tell the doctor about our little problem with your fantasies."

Some barely audible words emerged from behind

her hands. He caught the phrase "slow and painful death" and smiled, satisfied.

"The truth is, she's a bit of an exhibitionist. The reason we haven't been doing much of anything in our bedroom is that it's too tame for her. She's not interested unless there is an element of danger. She just keeps getting more and more adventurous...and nothing else will do. It's just a matter of time until we get ourselves arrested."

"I see." The doctor stared at the top of Joanna's head for a while, before turning his attention back to Matt. He nodded slowly. "I see. This is indeed a problem."

"It is," Matt confirmed. "Quite a problem."

"Indeed." Dr. Walters was silent for a long moment, staring hard at Jo. Then he switched his gaze to Matt. "And your inability to fulfill your wife's fantasies, are they only mental hang-ups, or do they lead to physical difficulties as well?"

"What?"

The doctor tapped his pen against his pad, his gaze disapproving. "You have an open-minded and free-spirited wife with a strong sensual nature, Matthew, while you yourself are stuck in another century. It's not uncommon for men to feel threatened in those circumstances and have problems with performing, even within their own inhibited parameters. Performance anxiety under those circumstances is understandable. The cure lies in working on loosening your own inhibitions."

This wasn't funny anymore. Then why were Jo's shoulders still shaking? She looked up and he could see her cheeks were wet with tears from laughing. "Matt, he does have a point. We can't let your inhibitions and hang-ups, your old-fashioned, narrow-minded view on sexuality ruin our marriage.''

Matt felt like baring his teeth at her and growling. She was in for a punishment. If only he could think of one grave enough. He stood up. ''Thank you, doctor, but that'll be all—will you send a bill? To Mrs. Brande,'' he added grimly.

''Certainly—would you like to book another appointment?''

''No,'' Matt said. ''I most definitely wouldn't.''

Jo wasn't in the living room when he got back. She'd probably escaped into her bedroom, hoping he wouldn't follow to tell her exactly what he thought of her little game.

Fat chance.

He headed for the stairs and took them two at a time. She'd pay for this.

She had dried her tears by the time he got there, and her face was almost back to normal, if you didn't count the chuckles that escaped every few seconds. She was sitting cross-legged on her bed, a pillow clutched to her chest, and her face was red.

He kicked the door shut with his heel and leaned against it, his arms crossed and his brow heavy. Jo had had her little joke, but now they had unfinished business.

''Well, I'm glad you got a kick out of this,'' he said. Jo put her hand over her mouth, but her giggles were still escaping. He shook his head. ''So you've got problems with my old-fashioned, narrow-minded sexuality, do you?''

Jo's words were muffled from behind her hand. ''You started it!'' she countered.

"Well, you certainly repaid me."

Jo lost control of her giggles for a few moments. "Lord, Matt, you should have seen your face when he was talking about your performance anxiety."

"Of course, you do know I don't have any problems."

Her grin turned mocking. It made him want to corner her and hold her imprisoned while he kissed it away. "Men. Just the mention of problems in that area frightens you, doesn't it? You really want my reassurance?" She inched backward on the bed, looking wary. "Why are you looking at me like that? Are you now going to jump me to prove your virility?"

Matt shook his head slowly and took a few steps forward, not losing eye contact for a second. "You have no idea how tempting that is. You deserve a good spanking."

There was humor in Joanna's eyes, an expression that he knew well, but hadn't seen for a long time. "Kinky, Matt. Dr. Walters would be proud." Her teasing grin was so familiar, and he'd missed it so much it brought an ache to his gut. "Well, you have to admit my 'complaints' have a basis in truth. You were never fond of affectionate displays in public."

Matt shook his head, the playfulness vanishing as he crashed back down to the grayness of reality and felt the weight of all that had happened settle on his shoulders. He straightened up and shook his head. "It wasn't because I didn't want to, Jo. We were trying to keep our relationship a secret. There was a reason. A good reason."

Her smile faded too. "I know."

She knew. But she didn't understand. She never had understood that he'd been trying to spare her. "I was your boss, Jo. I was trying to protect you until we could figure something out.''

"Yeah. And a great job you did at protecting me."

He closed his eyes. "Jo…"

"Sorry. I do seem to have trouble with the forgetting and forgiving part, don't I?"

Her voice was flip, but the smile had gone from her eyes, replaced by the hard defense he was so used to seeing. He'd hurt her badly. He hadn't even realized how badly. Maybe there really was no hope of salvaging what they'd had.

There had to be.

Before he could change his mind, he'd crossed the floor in a heartbeat, reached out for her hand and pulled her to her feet. He noticed the startled look on her face only for a second before he had his hands cupping her face and his mouth drinking from hers. She didn't even hesitate before responding, which warmed his heart and promised him that there might be hope for them after all. The kiss was as hot and deep as ever, her breath sweet and her skin warm against his hands. But there was something wrong…

Her hair…it should be flowing over his fingers, should be warm and vibrant and alive, but it was gone. Her lips were the same, soft and yielding, and her scent was the same….

But he couldn't forget her hair—and his suspicions of why it was gone.

He rested his forehead against hers and stared into her eyes, imprisoning her hands in his and holding them against his heart. She tried to free them, shock in her eyes now at what they'd just done, but he tightened his hold. "Tell me, Jo. Why did you cut your hair?"

Her eyes flickered. "Why not? It's fashionable, you know. This is *in*. And I was in the mood for a change anyway."

"A change?"

"Yes. I wanted something different. It's comfortable this short. No problem to maintain. I like it. I *love* it," she added, so defiantly that it convinced him she hated it herself.

He trailed a finger up her neck, past the outline of her ear and brushed it through the short wisps. "Your hair was so beautiful, Jo," he said. "Perfect."

Her eyes filled with tears and at the same time she pushed her elbow against his gut and shoved him away. "It's none of your business, Matt. Nothing I do is any of your business. Not anymore."

He grabbed her hands and imprisoned them against his chest again, pinning her against the wall. "Tell me the truth about why you cut your hair, Jo."

"I just did, Matt! Let go of me."

"You lied. Tell me the real reason."

"Because you loved it so much," she shouted, finally looking up at him again, tears sliding from her eyes as she blinked in angry defiance and her body slackened in defeat. "Yes! I cut my hair because of you! Happy now?"

"No," he said and let her go, feeling ashamed and depressed at having forced the words out of her. "I'm not happy."

She stared at him for a moment and when she spoke, her words almost stumbled out of her. "Let's go talk to Grandma. Now. We'll tell her everything. This has to end." Her voice broke on the last word. "I can't handle this anymore. Let's tell her right now."

He touched his thumb to her lower lip, then to her flushed cheeks. Her eyes were shimmering with emotion. He hated to see her so miserable. "I don't think now would be a good time, Jo," he whispered, not wanting to hurt her more, but she wouldn't want Esther to see her in this state. "Your face. It shows that you've been kissing and crying."

Jo gave a sharp sound of fury as she pushed his hand away. She stalked past him and out of the room, slamming the bathroom door behind her.

She'd cut her hair because of him. It was only confirmation of what he'd thought—a confirmation of how much their relationship had meant to her. But things were not exactly looking up regarding reconciliation, were they?

Matt took a deep breath, shook his head and headed toward Esther's room. The old lady needed a good talking-to—but at least the whole farce had made Jo laugh before he had made her cry. Her laughter was a sound he'd missed.

Esther was in her easy chair, crossword puzzle in hand, the dogs resting at her feet and an audio book on the stereo. Matt pushed the pause button and knelt in front of his godmother, pushing one sleeping dog out of the way. She raised an eyebrow in question, her eyes twinkling. "Hello, Matt. Did the therapist help?"

Matt sighed. "Esther…"

"Yes, love?"

"Jo and I do not need a sex therapist."

Esther winced. "He's a marital relations counselor. There's no need to be crude."

Matt put the puzzle book on the table and grabbed both her hands. "Esther, you know you're my favorite person in the world, but if you ever again try to interfere with my...marital relations, one of these days you're going to wake up and find that your hair has been dyed orange.''

Esther's lips pursed in a pout that reminded him of Jo during happier times. ''I just wanted to help, Matthew. You didn't spend your wedding night together. It's obvious that you're having problems.''

''Not that kind of problem. We do fine in that department. We always have.'' Matt closed his eyes, not believing he'd had to confide this to his godmother.

Esther was eyeing him suspiciously when he opened his eyes again. ''So you were having marital relations before the marriage, eh?''

''Well, people do, these days. It's the way of things.''

''Well, to be truthful, they also did sixty years ago,'' she whispered.

He tried to look properly scandalized, as he was expected to. ''Esther!''

Esther cackled. ''Don't tell Jo. She's bound to check the date of her mother's birth and my wedding date. Not something I recommend. She's so serious these days. She'd probably put 'grand-bastard' on her résumé.''

'' 'Grand-bastard'?'' Esther was good at making his head spin in confusion. It was an ability her granddaughter had inherited.

''Well, if everything's fine in that department, you should sleep in the same room. Don't give me that crap about you snoring. A woman wouldn't let a few snores keep her away from the man she loves.''

Matt stared at his godmother, saw the concern in her eyes, and the pieces fell into place. He *had* been manipulated after all—more than he'd realized. "You know," he said. "Don't you? You know *everything.*"

Esther fiddled with her pencil. "Isn't Jo waiting for you?"

"The game is up, Esther." He shook his head. "I was convinced you were exaggerating things to get us into a marriage, but that's not all, is it? You knew we'd broken up. Jo never told you—and you used that against us."

"Well, breaking up was a stupid move, if you ask me."

"It wasn't my choice. It was Jo's decision."

"And you just let her?"

"What was I supposed to do, grab her by the hair and drag her back to my cave?"

"Absolutely. Figuratively speaking, of course." Esther was frowning now. "Do you think Jo realizes what I was up to?"

Matt shook his head. "No. She's pretty sure that you exaggerated things to get us married, but she doesn't suspect you know we broke up." He sent her a harsh glare. "She doesn't believe you capable of such duplicity."

Esther failed to look guilty. "Why do so many people assume you're above suspicion when you're old?" she mused. "A whole lifetime of debauchery and sin, and people assume you don't even know the real story of the birds and the bees."

"A lifetime of debauchery and sin?"

Esther gave him a quirky smile. "Exaggeration is an old lady's prerogative, isn't it?"

He chuckled. "Of course."

"You're perfect for each other. That's why I pretended to be a bit under the weather..."

"*A bit under the weather?* You told us you were dying!"

Esther ignored him. "...and pushed for the marriage. I waited and waited and you obviously weren't about to make up. You had problems—and you let that be the end of it." She shook her head in disgust. "Young people today have no stamina to try to work out their problems."

"I see. That's why you did it."

"Yes. If you were married, if you were forced to be together, you'd have to work out your problems instead of running away from them."

Matt tilted his head and stared at his godmother. Jo would go ballistic when she found out. "First, this wasn't a legally binding marriage, Esther, and although we were pretending in front of you, it was never a real marriage to us. Second, there is such a thing as divorce."

"You two won't divorce," Esther dismissed.

"What makes you so sure?"

"Why, you're in love." She narrowed her eyes and shook his hand. "Aren't you? You do want Joanna back, don't you?"

Matt sighed. "Yes. I want her back. That's probably why I was stupid enough to let you trick us into this marriage." He was silent for a moment, thinking. "Esther, I don't approve of what you did, and I hope you never do that again, but maybe we can make this work to our advantage." He took his grandmother's hand and squeezed. "The important thing is that you don't tell Jo yet."

"Don't tell Jo what?"

She was standing in the doorway, brimming with suspicion. Her face no longer bore the marks of either kissing or crying, and Matt saw determination in her face that spelled trouble. If he didn't do something to prevent it, she would tell Esther the truth now and it would be over. "What are you two up to?"

Esther sighed. "I was confessing, love."

Matt turned his head, staring at his godmother. She too? No. Esther couldn't confess to Jo, not just yet. That would mean the end of everything—and he was just getting started. He'd kissed Jo again—and now there was nothing that would stop him in his mission of getting her back. He stood up, blocking Esther's view of Joanna, and managed to give her a warning gesture without Jo seeing. Esther's eyes widened and she nodded once in understanding. He turned around and sent the same warning gesture to Jo, who raised her eyebrows in question, but gave a slight nod that told him she would play along until he explained.

"Your grandmother just bought us a honeymoon," he told Jo. "It was meant to be a surprise."

"A honeymoon?" Jo leaned against the doorway, turning pale. Her eyes were full of questions, but he had no choice but to ignore them for now. He'd figure out some kind of explanation—only he'd have to do it fast.

Esther caught on quickly. "Yes. I deprived you of a real wedding, so I'm giving you a honeymoon to make up for it a bit. I handpicked the spot. You'll love it."

"Where is it?" Jo asked, obviously stalling for time. Her eyes kept sending desperate messages to him, and he threw her a tiny shrug in return. "Where…?"

Esther opened her mouth, looking confused. Matt bent down and hugged the old lady, whispering

"Leave it to me," into her ear. "Thank you, Esther," he then said aloud, explaining away the sudden hug.

"It's a mountain cottage," he told Jo. "Esther already told me all about it, and it sounds wonderful. Amazing view, isolated. Perfect privacy."

"An outdoor tub," Esther chimed in—and he added that to his mental list. He'd better find such a place. And soon, before Jo found a way to wriggle out of this.

"We leave Saturday morning," he said.

"I see." Jo shook her head. "But I can't leave, not on such a short notice. I can't possibly go. I can't take time off work."

"It's just a long weekend, so you only need one day off. Esther already called your boss," he lied blatantly. He'd call Carl later and fix it. "He's more than willing to give you Monday off and was thrilled to hear about the wedding."

Inwardly he was wincing at the mounting pile of lies. Was this really the way to get Jo back?

"You called my boss?" Jo whispered. "Grandma…"

"He didn't know you were married," Esther happily told her. "Guess that man must be blind not to notice a new ring."

"I don't see him much," Jo muttered. Her eyes were pleading with Matt, but she wasn't giving anything away.

Good. She wanted his cooperation, and she wouldn't be getting it. No way.

Jo walked to Esther's bed, and grabbed her grandmother's hand. "Grandma, there's no way we're leaving you alone here in your condition."

"My *condition* is fine," Esther said, reminding him

of her trickery and Jo's misery over it. It had been cruel of Esther, even if she'd had the best intentions.

"I thought you were dying," he said.

"Matt!" Somehow Jo managed to hiss his name although it didn't have a single sibilant in it. Impressive.

Esther seemed less offended by his dry comment than Jo was. "Well, I promise not to die tonight, don't worry."

"Grandma, I'm not leaving you," Jo said firmly.

"The girls are staying while you're away," Esther told her. "All three of them. We're going to have late nights and all-night bridge games. How many people do you suppose have sleepovers in their eighties? Go on your honeymoon, Jo, and enjoy it."

"Grandma, I really appreciate your gesture... but..." She glanced up at Matt. "Would you talk to me for a minute?" She didn't wait for an answer, but left the room.

"You're really going on a honeymoon?" Esther asked, keeping her voice down. Matt nodded.

"Yeah."

"And you're going to be all macho and win her back, aren't you?"

"I'll do my best," he promised.

"How are you going to convince her to go?"

"I have my ways."

"I'm sure you do," Esther said with a smile.

Jo was cleaning the kitchen cupboards. In the minute she'd waited for him, she'd managed to empty out an entire cupboard and was halfway inside it with her sleeves rolled up. He remembered that trait of hers. She'd always used housework to work off the angry energy she wouldn't release elsewhere. "I can't believe she called my boss,'' she growled when she noticed he was here. "I have to call him and apologize.''

She started toward the phone, and he tried desperately to think of something to slow her down. He'd have to reach Carl before she did. "Don't worry. It'll be fine," he said, stepping between her and the phone.

She glared at him. "Fine? We have to tell her. Right now. I wanted to tell her today—you'd better have a good reason for stopping me. There is no way I'm going to pretend to go on a honeymoon on top of pretending to marry you."

"Pretend honeymoon," he mused. "It's a fascinating concept, isn't it?"

"You mean we pretend to go?" She shook her head. "We can't do that, even if we wanted to. She's going to want pictures, a postcard, details of how that cottage looks. Are you suggesting we forge all that? And why?"

"We could always tell her we spent the whole weekend in bed and didn't notice anything but each other."

She paused in her cleaning, her hand moving in a gesture from when her hair was long, an attempt to push it out of her eyes. When her hand didn't encounter strands of hair, she rubbed at her temple instead. He smiled at the thought, and her eyes narrowed. "You're not finding this funny, are you, Matt?"

"It *is* funny."

"Under other circumstances it might be funny…"

He was infuriating. Didn't this hurt him at all? It was agony for her, with all she still felt for him, to pretend she was married—and now she'd have to go on a pretend honeymoon? And he still hadn't explained why, for heaven's sake. They were just postponing the inevitable.

"We have to reach a decision, Matt. This can't go on forever. Grandma is doing fine now. We're not going to keep up this pretence for years, are we?"

"I suppose it would be tricky—after the pretend honeymoon, there'd be a pretend pregnancy, then a pretend birth and a pretend baby…at which time she'd probably catch on."

Jo stared into the newly cleaned cabinet. Her own apartment had been spotless ever since she'd broken up with Matt. It beat any therapy. "Would you please be serious about this?" she snapped. Her heart still hadn't recovered after their kiss, after that outburst of emotion on both sides. Matt knew she'd cut her hair because of him. He knew she'd loved him.

"Am I smiling?"

She checked. He wasn't. Not anymore, anyway. "No." She slammed the cabinet door shut and headed for the coffee. This had gone way out of hand and it was time to end it. "This is it. We tell her now. One cup of strong coffee, then we tell her."

Matt squirmed into a kitchen chair opposite her—and the kitchen felt way too small. "No. I have a better idea about how to break it to her."

"I'm listening. This better be good."

"We'll go on that pretend honeymoon—at least we'll be in peace for a few days, no Esther trying to push us into bed together. Maybe when we get away from everything, some magic solution will present itself. If not…" He took a deep breath. "If we decide at the end of the weekend that there is no other way, we'll come back and tell people our marriage was a mistake and that we're getting a divorce.''

A divorce? "Why? Why a divorce? Why not just tell them the truth? And tell them now?''

"The truth will make Esther look like a fool. And if we go with the divorce story now, it's too sudden.'' He shrugged. "But after a honeymoon, several days of just the two of us in close proximity—I bet plenty of couples suddenly realize they can't stand each other. It's a good enough excuse, anyway.''

Jo stared at him, biting her lip. "Cynical, but you do have a point. This might make it easier on everybody. We'd just break up, naturally, amicably, and after that we never need to see each other again.''

"Right.'' It wasn't going to happen, he vowed. He'd convince Jo they had a future together. There was still the small matter of letting her know that her reputation had been cleared—but that had to wait. He couldn't lose this chance. First, there was a pretend honeymoon to turn into a real one. Then—the truth could come out. One long weekend—one chance to win back what they'd lost. He'd make it work.

Jo looked up at him, determination in her jawline, although it was pretty clear her goals for this weekend were not the same as his. "Terrific. When can we leave on our divorcemoon?''

Great. Now she couldn't wait.

CHAPTER SEVEN

"PRETEND divorce, here we come," Jo sighed, resting her head back as they finally got out on the freeway, heading for the mountains that seemed much farther away than they really were. They were off to a late start and Matt suspected it was deliberate—she was trying to shorten the weekend. He sent her a look.

"Can't wait to be a free woman again, can you?"

"No."

Something clawed at his heart as it occurred to him for the first time that there might be someone else already. Could it be? "Why? Are you seeing someone? Someone who isn't happy about this?"

She turned her face and he felt her gaze bite into his temple. "It's only been six weeks since we broke up, Matt. And if I were seeing someone, do you really think I'd have agreed to this fake marriage—let alone gone on a pretend honeymoon with you?"

"No, I suppose not," he conceded. "No guy in his right mind would allow you to go on a pretend honeymoon with someone else. Sorry."

She snorted and tossed her head in a way that reminded him of her lost hair. "There you go again. *Allow.* Sometimes you're incredibly old-fashioned, Matt."

"It goes both ways," he defended himself. "I wouldn't want my woman to *allow* me to go on a honeymoon with someone either."

"So I suppose that means you're not seeing anyone either?"

Casual indifference in her voice, and his hands tightened on the wheel. "Of course not. We just broke up."

"It's been six whole weeks."

He grinned at her, but it was forced. "When we were talking about *you,* you said it's 'only' been six weeks. Why the difference?"

"It *is* different for men. The way some guys act, it seems your masculinity is threatened if you haven't been to bed with someone for a whole week."

"Well..." he glanced at his watch. "It's been six weeks, two days and twenty hours, and nothing's shriveled up and died so far."

Out of the corner of his eye he saw Jo blush slightly, and now she could no longer flick her hair in front of her face to hide it. She might not want to remember what they'd been doing six weeks, two days and twenty hours ago, but she did. So did he. In vivid detail.

"Congratulations," she said dryly, looking out the side window, away from him. "I'll take your word for it."

"Feels like it's been a lot more than six weeks," he remarked after a heavy silence.

"Time's relative, they say," Jo muttered. She was obviously coming to the conclusion that this hadn't been the brightest idea in the world. She fidgeted in her seat, even twisted around to look with longing back to the city.

"Something wrong?" Matt asked, picking up speed a bit. He wasn't turning around now. No way.

"Maybe this wasn't a good idea."

"It was the best one I could come up with."

"We don't actually have to go to that cabin, you know. Why don't we just go home? To our respective homes, I mean. When we tell everybody we broke up on our honeymoon, they're not going to be asking for pictures and postcards. There's no need to actually go."

Matt felt his heart pick up speed. She wasn't going to sabotage the brightest idea he'd had in…six weeks, was she? "We're halfway there already, Jo. Why not just go through with it, and look at it as a vacation? It's not that often you're offered a free vacation at a luxury cottage in the mountains, is it? And it'll make it easier to answer Esther's questions when we get back."

Jo kept squirming in her seat. "How can we possibly look upon it as a vacation if we're together?"

"Is it really that terrible to be around me?"

Without turning his head he felt the force of her glare. "What kind of a question is that? It does tend to be rather painful—at the very least uncomfortable—to be around your ex just after you've broken up!" She folded her arms and stared straight ahead again. "Obviously, it's no big deal for you. No surprise there. Fits the picture."

Matt shook his head. "I don't know where you got the idea that our relationship meant so little to me."

Jo shrugged. "Was it ever a 'relationship'? Nobody knew, except Grandma. You didn't want anybody to know."

"Do you really think I'd have included Esther in this if it didn't mean something to me? The only reason I didn't want other people to know was because of work. It's not easy for a junior staff member to be dating the CEO. Hell, it's against company policy. Of course I wanted to keep it a secret.''

''But you never...''

Matt swiveled his head toward her impatiently when she didn't continue. ''Never what?''

She sighed and shook her head. You did not say to a man a month after you broke up *But you never said you loved me.* ''Apart from the whole suspension issue—you didn't even understand why I didn't want you to plant me in another job when I left, why I wanted to do that on my own.''

''What's the big deal? I got you your first job with me, and you didn't freak out then.''

''Of course I didn't freak out. But that was different. You weren't my...'' She waved a hand irritably. ''My *whatever,* back then. But I still didn't like it. Do you think I was happy with having you take me on originally as a favor to my grandmother?''

Matt shook his head. ''Most people get jobs through some sort of a connection. It doesn't mean they're any less deserving or capable.''

''You stuck me in a brainless position! I was essentially moving piles of papers from one end of the office to the other!''

Matt grimaced. ''Well, if you knew what some of the kids I've hired out of college have gotten up to at my workplace, you wouldn't be surprised I had trouble trusting new employees. You got a promotion as soon as you'd shown what you were capable of.''

''Did I?''

''Did you what?''

''Did I get the promotion because I deserved it?''

Matt's profile looked blank, then he glanced at her

sideways, looking confused. "Of course you did. Why else would you get a promotion?"

"I don't know. Why else?"

Matt stared at her, silent for a moment. "I see. That's been biting at you all this time?"

She squirmed. "Well...yes."

Unexpectedly Matt grinned. "You got the promotion because you deserved it. I started chasing after you, despite company policy and my better judgment, because I couldn't help myself."

"Oh."

He was stealing glances at her again, but she kept her own eyes firmly on the road—as he should be doing. "I wouldn't be much of a businessman, Jo, if I let my heart choose my employees."

Just a figure of speech, Joanna yelled at her own heart, silly enough to start galloping at this news.

She still loved him, didn't she? Not only was she not "over him," she was still in love.

The discovery blurred her vision and made her deaf for a long while as she stared out the window, feeling almost sick. Matt's touch on her knee woke her up at last. "You okay?"

"Yeah. Would you keep your eyes on the road, Matt? I'm fine. Just thinking. I hate to leave Grandma," she added after a small pause. Grandma. She'd keep her concentration on the old lady, either to worry about her or be furious with her. It didn't matter. Just as long as she kept her focus on Grandma and not on herself and Matt.

"She'll be fine. We've got our cell phones, we can check up on her whenever we want to. She's got three people—at least—staying with her."

"How do you think she'll take our 'divorce'?"

"She won't like it, that's a given."

"Yeah. But I think it will be fine. It *has* to be fine. We probably need to break it to her gently, stress that we're still friends, still like each other, but just aren't suited to be man and wife..."

"Careful what you say. Don't mention incompatibility or she might sic the sex therapist on us again."

Jo laughed, then covered her face with her hands and shook her head. "Oh, Matt—can you believe it?"

"I'll never recover," he told her.

Jo rested her head against the side window and giggled. She looked at Matt sideways, and he was looking at the road, smiling. She half closed her eyes, and kept looking at him. Whoever said men couldn't be beautiful had a warped meaning of the word.

And it was so good to see him laugh.

She closed her eyes completely as the pain set in again.

How was she going to last for a long weekend in a romantic honeymoon cottage—alone with him?

Jo fell asleep on the way, her head lolling against the window, her hands loosely clasped in her lap. Matt tried to keep his driving smooth enough not to wake her, but when they got onto the potholed road leading to the cottages, the bumps woke her up. She stretched, a movement that tempted him far too much, and looked around.

"We're almost there," he told her. "Just twenty more minutes or so."

"It's gorgeous here," Jo said, staring wide-eyed at the view, after rubbing her eyes like a sleepy child. "Grandma sure knows how to pick honeymoon spots. I didn't know she'd ever been here."

Matt winced. Finding the right place had been a nightmare, but with the frantic work of several travel agents, he'd managed to locate a cottage that had all the trimmings Esther had given her imaginary one.

They finally pulled up at their destination, and Jo jumped out of the car as soon as it came to a stop. He wasn't sure if it was to escape him, or to take a closer look at the cottage, but either way he didn't blame her. He got out himself, dug the keys to the cottage out of a pocket, and got their suitcases out of the trunk. Jo was staring around with an awed expression. The view was even more magnificent out of the car, with no dirty windshield to dampen the experience.

The cottage was no less impressive, at least not from the outside. It wasn't big, but it looked lovely, and it should have all conveniences, including the outdoor tub Esther had again insisted upon. That amenity had made it particularly difficult to find a cottage that suited Esther's fantasy.

"Want to take a look inside?" he asked, and Jo smiled.

"I don't know. It looks so wonderful from the outside, I'm almost afraid to."

He unlocked the door, and waited for her to step in.

Phase two of Getting Jo Back had begun.

Jo took one look at the romantic inside of the cottage and then fled out to the balcony, clutching the banister and grinding her teeth to keep herself from hyperventilating. She'd never last three days here alone with Matt. Not without some serious damage to her heart and spirit.

What had she been thinking? What had *they* been thinking?

She shook her head, trying to rid her mind of the panic and stared out over the valley below. She was here. It was done.

Maybe they could just return tomorrow, instead of staying the entire time. Yeah, that'd be better. Take a few snapshots for Esther and go back to the city to get the fake divorce. She could survive twenty-four hours with Matt, couldn't she?

The view down the mountain was amazing—the trees and the rocks forming a perfect symphony of green and gray. She looked up at the blue skies, thinking that the only thing to rival that view might be the night sky. She tried to remember when she'd last seen the night sky outside the city. Probably not since she was a child, camping with her parents on one of their infrequent attempts at family bonding.

She heard Matt come up behind her, and saw his arms brace themselves on the railing. She didn't look to her side, but she felt his presence in every cell. ''This is a lovely place,'' she whispered. It was impossible not to whisper here. ''It would be perfect for a real honeymoon.''

''Yes.''

She leaned on the balcony. ''It's so quiet. When you're living in a city, you stop noticing that it's never fully quiet. There's always some sound. Here there is real silence.''

He didn't reply, but she could almost hear him nod in agreement.

Then he was touching her.

Jo stood absolutely still, wondering what his hand was doing on her arm. His thumb stroked the bare skin on the inside of her forearm, and she realized she was holding her breath. "Matt?" she asked, in an explosion of a whisper, but still did not dare look at him.

"Yes?" he asked.

"Why are you touching me?"

"You dislike it?"

She pulled away, but didn't look at him until she was safely a few steps away. "I don't dislike it. But I don't play games. What's going on?"

Matt was still leaning on the railing, but there was a warm calm glow in his eyes. "It was all a mistake, wasn't it?"

"What was?"

"The mess at the company. Breaking up. All the misunderstanding and stupid pride that broke us up. There was no good reason."

"Trust. That's a good reason. You didn't trust me."

"Ditto," he said softly. "You didn't trust me. You don't trust anyone, do you?"

"What do you mean? I'm not untrusting."

"Yes you are. And I don't blame you. You could never count on your parents—and now you won't allow yourself to count on anyone. One suspicion that I might have let you down, and you ran away and didn't even give me a chance."

"Don't psychoanalyze me."

"I don't have the training for that, Jo, but it's obvious."

"I did trust you. I waited for you, I didn't spill about our relationship because I was waiting for you. Hoping you could make it right."

"And when I did something other than what you

expected—you ran without giving me a chance to do things my way. Your trust was only provisional.''

She raised her gaze toward the ceiling and gave an exaggerated grimace. ''Great, now you're talking in lawyer-speak on top of the psychobabble.''

''Do you honestly believe there is no truth in this?'' he asked.

Jo rubbed her face with her hands, tired, too tired to think about what he was saying, but his words had nevertheless taken root somewhere deep in her mind. Could he be right? Had she let some stupid childhood issues influence something so important? He was right that she'd never been able to count on her parents—but she hadn't transferred that to *Matt*, had she? ''We're never going to agree on this.''

''What do you say we forget about it, then? And try to do better in the future?''

''We can't do that.''

''Okay,'' he said impatiently. ''Fine. Let's not forget it. Let's deal with it until it's dead, and then we'll be free of it.''

''Matt…do you really want to rehash something that was painful and horrible for both of us?''

''No. I don't want to rehash it, I want us to get over it and move on.''

''We have moved on. We're past it. We're over it. We're over each other.''

''Really?'' His eyes narrowed and his gaze was laser sharp. ''We're over each other? Is that why we can't even breathe normally when we're in a room together?''

She stared at him, breath caught in her throat to prove his point. He was right. She did have trouble breathing around him. For the longest time she'd managed to deceive herself that it was no longer because of the sensual pull between them, only because of anger and resentment—but it wasn't true.

She'd never before known he'd had trouble breathing around her, and that news was as fascinating as it was frightening.

"Breathe normally...?" she asked, stalling, and he stepped closer, again proving his point. Scent of leather, soap—*Matt*.

Oh, no. Now her knees were turning weak.

She *hated* it when that happened.

He touched her upper arms with the flats of his palms, just barely. "Yes—and when we touch... breathing is very low on my list of priorities. Don't you know that? You have to know *that*, at least."

She stepped back, but even when she was against the wall, his hand was still on her arm. She desperately reminded herself of why they were here in the first place—of everything that had happened. They wouldn't even have met again if it wasn't for Grandma and her health problems. Why did he keep making it about *them?* "We don't even have trust, Matt. Trust is the foundation of every relationship. If we don't have that, we have nothing."

Matt's hand finally dropped and he looked away, staring at the view again. His shoulders had drooped in defeat and she ached to go to him. "Why are you so stubborn, Jo?"

"Inborn trait," she quipped. There was relief that he wasn't touching her anymore—but she was all too aware of her breathing difficulties, now that he'd brought it up. "Just look at Grandma."

"Doesn't everybody deserve a second chance?"

Jo bit her lip. Yes. He was right. Everybody deserved a second chance. "Yes," she whispered, and Matt's head snapped back, eyes dark in disbelief and hope.

"Jo...?"

She held up a hand. "We have a truce this weekend, okay? We'll just take it easy and see what happens. Maybe we can get a second chance...but I don't want to rush into anything just because..."

"Just because what?"

"Just because we're still lusting after each other," she admitted gruffly, and Matt's laugh was loud enough to echo in the mountains. She turned away to hide her own grin, the release of tension welcome. "That's not funny," she reprimanded him.

"Well, we only have one bed."

She rolled her eyes. "I know. This is a honeymoon cottage. That's why we brought the air mattress, remember?"

"I do remember. I was just hoping *you'd* forgotten."

Playful. She could take a playful and teasing Matt, couldn't she? Or would she just get her heart in even deeper trouble? "No such luck, buster. I remember."

Matt sighed theatrically. "You're really going to make me sleep on the air mattress when we have a pink heart-shaped bed to sleep in?"

"Pink heart-shaped bed?" Jo repeated, and shot back into the cottage and into the bedroom. He didn't follow, and she returned to the balcony after a good hard stare at a bed that was neither pink nor heart-shaped. "You were joking."

"Of course I was joking. Esther's taste isn't quite that bad."

Jo leaned on the balcony railing again. "So, what are we going to do while we're here? Besides stare at the scenery, of course?"

Matt shrugged. "I don't know. What do people usually do on their honeymoons?"

She gave him a wry glance, which he returned with the most innocent green stare she'd ever seen. "Catch up on their reading?"

"My laptop is out in the car. I can always do some work, I guess."

She groaned. "Matt—a word of advice: when you go on a real honeymoon, don't bring your laptop."

He grinned. "You hate my laptop, don't you?"

"I don't hate your laptop. I used to be slightly annoyed at all the attention it would get."

Matt grinned lopsidedly. "I loved the methods you used to regain my attention."

She stared at him suspiciously, and his grin widened. "Matt, you mean…no." She shook her head. "You didn't do it on purpose. I don't believe it."

He kept grinning at her. "I'm a quick study. When I found out all I had to do was turn on the computer and you'd be right there in my lap, obscuring the screen…." His grin was wistful, and it melted her. "Well…it worked."

"There are other ways to get me into your arms, you know."

She'd said *are*. Not *were*. She wouldn't correct it— that would just draw attention to it. She'd have to watch out for these kinds of slips. Things were rapidly sliding back to the way they had been—and it wasn't safe.

"I know. But that one has always been my favorite."

"Sneaky. It's not going to work now that I know about it," she warned him. "I mean—it wouldn't. If we were still... Hell."

Matt tapped her shoulder as she turned her back on him, and then his arms came around her from behind, hugging her close, but carefully. Then he let go, and she felt alone. "Don't think too much, Jo. Second chances, wasn't that the deal?"

"Second chances," she agreed, trying to resist the temptation to go to him for a second hug.

Why had he let her go so quickly?

CHAPTER EIGHT

MATT worked for the rest of the afternoon, and Jo curled up in a chair on the balcony, reading, her back to him. The temptation to distract him as she used to do was far too great—no need to complicate things by having him in her line of vision. Second chances—yes, and there was optimism and hope in the air, but rushing things wouldn't help any.

When it was time for dinner, they collaborated on figuring out how the barbecue worked, then ate inside as it was getting dark already. The conversation was easy, the mood light—but Jo was very aware that they were both working hard to keep it that way. It didn't come naturally.

When the food was long gone and the conversation had died out they just sat there, staring into the flickering embers of the fire for the longest time.

Then Matt stood up and walked to the window. He gave an exclamation of surprise, then held out a hand for her to join him. "Come on, Jo, have a look."

She walked toward him and he put his arm around her shoulders as he pointed upward. "Look."

The sky above was breathtaking. "Wow. They really are infinite, aren't they?"

"Hmmmm. Would you like to go out there?"

"Are you offering to take me?"

Matt chuckled. "That'd be original. A honeymoon in space. Seriously, would you want to go?"

She glanced at him, not sure if he was joking. "What do you mean? To the stars?"

"Yes."

She shrugged, enjoying the heavy weight of his arm around her shoulders. "If I were living in the twenty-seventh century, then yes, I would be tempted to take a cosmic voyage."

"Yeah. Maybe colonize a planet."

Jo chuckled. "Not me. That'd be hard work. I'd rather visit when they've installed plumbing and gotten rid of the toxins in the atmosphere."

Matt grinned down at her before looking up toward the stars again. "You were never a science fiction fan, were you?"

"Science fiction is for dreamers."

"You're not a dreamer?"

"I like reality."

"Why?"

She should pull away from him. Being so close wasn't good for her. "Dreams are just precursors to disappointment. You know where you stand with reality."

Matt turned her around and pushed at her chin until she met his eyes. "Reality is for those who can't handle fantasy. Haven't you ever heard that?"

His eyes were vivid, his face vibrant in the shadows from the fire. "Is that what this honeymoon is?" she whispered. "A fantasy?"

"It can be."

His chest was warm under her hands—originally there to hold him away, but now his heartbeat was pushing at her palm and she couldn't seem to move. She lowered her head, but his hand came up, holding her chin steady.

"What's wrong with having a fantasy, Jo?"

Now his body was warm against her front, and she hesitantly slipped her hand around his neck, to the back of his head where she'd always liked to play with his hair. Why was she doing this? How had he dragged her into his fantasy when she was so sure she'd rather cling to reality? "Just what sort of a fantasy would it be? One with indoor plumbing?"

He smiled. "Yes. Even a hot tub."

"Fantasy…"

"Our fantasy."

Despite her better judgment, she pushed her fingers between the buttons on his shirt to feel his warm flesh. She *needed* to. "Fantasies are transient, Matt. Untrustworthy, unreliable. They vanish when reality notices they're there and decides to do something about it."

"Yes…but while they last…" Matt murmured.

"Then what…?"

"Then they're wonderful."

But they don't last, she wanted to say, but she couldn't bear to hear herself say it. Instead she raised her gaze, stared at his mouth for a while before daring to meet the blaze of his eyes.

There was no reality there. Just heat, intense heat and certainty that drew her into his fantasy. His heart was pounding against her fingers and it was so right. She could feel the heat emanating from his lips. He was only inches away but it felt like miles. His arms were at his sides instead of being around her, and the absence was almost a physical pain.

"Matt…" she whispered, but couldn't even hear her own voice over the roaring of blood in her ears. She needed his touch, she needed to feel his arms around her, but he wasn't complying. Why not? Why wasn't he touching her when she *needed* him to?

Matt was almost trembling. He wanted to touch her so badly, but did he really want to drag her into a fantasy when she was so unsure they could even function in the same reality? Just a moment ago he'd been certain—but maybe he'd just end up hurting her even more.

But her skin was so soft. He touched her cheek, tapped at the corner of her mouth with his thumb. Her eyes fluttered shut then, and it became impossible for him to resist.

Her lips were soft, welcoming, warm—it felt like a homecoming until he slid his hand around to her hair and reality threatened to rip his fantasy apart. But her lips were opening against his and she was leaning into him, her arms going around him, and it was like a memory, a memory he'd thought he would never relive.

How could they have lost this? He didn't think he'd forgotten anything, not how her body felt pressed against his, not the taste of her lips or the tiny sounds she made when she wanted more, craved more. And she wanted him, she wanted his touch, she wanted his kisses, she wanted *him*. Not everything was lost. He had not killed what she had felt for him. The relief made him smile against her mouth and she smiled back, her lips curving, almost breaking the kiss and he growled and gently bit at her lower lip in a playful punishment.

She giggled, and he laughed himself, feeling an unexpected freedom in the joy, and he whispered into her ear. No sweet nothings, nothing intense or profound, just a stupid childish joke he'd told her dozens of times before.

"Don't, Matt." Like a little girl she was holding her hands over her mouth, trying not to laugh. "I can't resist it when you try to make me laugh with your horrid jokes."

"Good."

"Why?"

"I don't want you to resist me."

"I'm on to you. You just want to escape sleeping on the air mattress."

His eyes glinted. "Don't you want to try out the outdoor tub?"

"Don't look so hopeful, I did bring a very demure bathing suit."

In her purse, left on a shelf just inside the front door, her cell phone beeped. They both jumped, then Jo raced to get it, worried something might have happened to Esther.

It wasn't Esther. It was the hesitant voice of someone who'd once been her friend.

"Christine?" Why in the world would Christine be calling her—one of the people who'd turned their backs on her, believing she was a criminal?

"I just…wanted to apologize," Christine said hesitantly. "I know it was unforgivable, to act the way I did—"

"What are you talking about?"

"Everybody knows now that you're innocent, Jo. Matt sent a global e-mail out, explained the results of the investigation." She paused. "He made most of us feel rather ashamed of how we'd treated you, too."

"Wait…" She turned around, and saw that Matt was out on the patio, experimenting with the controls on the tub. She hurried into the bedroom and shut the door, just in case. "Christine, Matt explained what?"

"You haven't heard?"

"Obviously not."

"Matt said he would be going straight to see you, to apologize on behalf of the firm…"

"I'm away," she told Christine, turning around and staring out through the window at Matt's car, dusty from the long drive. "I'm away for a long weekend. I suppose he tried my home number or my office number, and I wasn't there."

"Oh. Oh! So I'm telling you the good news?" Christine perked up at this. "Everybody knows you didn't do it, Jo. We'll be groveling for months, I promise."

"Really?"

"Yes. We're sorry—we all are."

Her head was spinning from all the new information. "Thanks, Christine."

"Will you be coming back? I know Matt intended to ask you to come back. The board wants you back too." Christine's voice turned dry. "Although their motives are probably linked to that huge settlement you'd no doubt win if you sued them."

"I don't know…"

"Well, I just wanted to apologize."

"It's okay. Thank you, Chris. I appreciate it."

Jo ended the phone call in a daze. Why hadn't he told her? Why wasn't he telling her? This was good news for everybody.

She left the phone on the nightstand and walked out on to the porch to Matt. He looked up and smiled when he saw her coming. "Well, at least this thing works if you do decide to try out the demure swimming suit. Hot water and all. Was that Esther on the phone?''

"No."

Matt nodded. She followed him with her gaze as he turned the water off again and covered the tub. He hadn't told her. Why?

There would be a good reason—for some reason she was sure there would be. She opened her mouth, and without a conscious decision, she told him. "It was Christine, from work. Remember Christine? I shared a cubicle with her before I got my own office?''

Matt held his breath, and her gaze, for a long moment. Then he seemed to relax, probably at not seeing fury in her eyes. It was what he'd expected, she could see that now. "I see."

"She told me everything."

"Then you know your name has been cleared."

"Yes."

"Everybody's hoping you'll decide to come back. But I understand if you don't want to."

"I'll have to think about it," she told him.

"You're not angry," he said.

She took a deep breath. "No."

"I thought you'd be."

"I'm not angry—because I trust you to have a good explanation."

Matt sat down on the edge of the tub and held out a hand. "You trust me?"

She took his hand and let him pull her closer. "Yes. Why didn't you tell me?"

His smile was crooked, almost embarrassed. "And if it doesn't count as a good excuse—then what?"

"Then I push you in."

Matt glanced down into the half-filled tub and was quick to jump to his feet. He pulled her inside the cottage instead, and pushed her on to the sofa. "I wasn't sure how to tell you," he said quickly. "You stuck so hard to the idea that I thought you were guilty. I was worried that you might think the only reason I said I wanted a second chance for us was because someone convinced me you were innocent. I don't know... I wanted to—get my chance first, get this weekend first. And then tell you."

"I see."

"So—are you going to throw me in the tub?"

"I don't think so."

Matt stared at her for a minute. "Does that mean I'm forgiven?"

"You hurt me," she said, almost soundlessly.

The words were so simple. Yet so dangerous. They held more of her emotions than anything she'd ever said to him before—they made her vulnerable. It seemed such an obvious thing, but this wasn't an admission she'd ever made before. And he seemed to realize that. He stared into her eyes for the longest time before slowly nodding.

"I know."

She found she'd been holding her breath, waiting for his answer.

He continued. "You hurt me too."

"I did?" It had never occurred to her, but the look in his eyes told her it was the truth.

"You didn't trust me. You didn't believe in me."

She moved restlessly, fiddled with the sleeves of her shirt, longing to object. But she needed to give him time to finish what he was saying.

"You wouldn't even consider that I might be trying to do what was best for you...what was best for us."

"You wouldn't even acknowledge that there *was* an us," she burst out, finally giving voice to the worst hurt of all. "Everything would have been okay if you'd just told people we were together."

"No, Jo." He approached her and she shrank back, simply because his presence was so powerful. He knelt by her side and took her hands in his, obviously intent on her absorbing every word. "We've talked about this before. It wouldn't have helped. It would have *hurt*. Me too—it wouldn't have helped my reputation with the board, but mainly it would have hurt you. The thief used my computer, my password. If it had come out that you were my...girlfriend, the suspicions would just have been even stronger." He sighed. "And when you wouldn't listen, my pride was hurt too—"

"I know, Matt," she interrupted. "I know now why you didn't tell them about us. But it was because you wouldn't acknowledge our relationship that I thought you didn't care..."

There was new understanding in his eyes. "We should have fought harder for each other, shouldn't we?"

"Yes."

"I'm sorry that I hurt you," he said.

She looked down, but then up again, bravely locking her gaze with his. "I hurt you too. I'm sorry."

"It's okay. It's over."

"We both made mistakes. I may have...overreacted," she admitted. "You tried to do the right thing..."

"Do you think we can start over?"

He'd moved closer by the time she looked up, and she couldn't help it—there were tears in her eyes. "I don't know, Matt."

"Because you don't trust me?"

"No...because..."

"Tell me."

Because I never knew exactly what you felt for me. I still don't know.

She couldn't say that. Pride wouldn't let her—pride and fear.

"Because it might happen again," she said instead. "We might hurt each other again."

He touched her cheek softly, and she couldn't help but reciprocate, reaching out to caress his cheekbone with the tips of her fingers. "We'll try not to," he whispered. "We'll try really hard not to. Okay?"

She was under his spell again, yet she didn't feel she'd lost a battle. She was winning. They both were. She leaned into his arms and burrowed into him, relaxing against his body. A smile bloomed inside her, but took quite a while to reach her face. When it did, she tilted her head back to show him, then buried her face again in his shoulder. "Yes," she said, the word muffled against his shirt, and she felt his mouth touch her temple. "We'll try really hard."

CHAPTER NINE

MATT opened his eyes grumbling about the terrible suffering he'd endured on his night on the air mattress and he kept complaining all the way through breakfast. She just smiled sweetly at him, and told him patience was a virtue.

Of course, she hadn't slept any better on the luxurious double bed. She'd tiptoed to the door more than once, tempted to join him on the uncomfortable air mattress—tempted to open the door and invite him to share her fancy honeymoon pillows.

But she'd resisted temptation. She was rather proud of that. Last night, she'd gotten way too wrapped up in his suggestive whispers of second chances and promises not to hurt each other again. Go slow. That had to be the motto here.

At least for now. She wasn't sure how long she would be able to stick to that motto.

Matt had melted back into the man he'd been during the time they'd dated. The grim exhaustion in his eyes had almost vanished, and when she walked barefoot to the kitchen without even giving him a morning kiss first, he resorted to his laptop trick, grinning at her with a teasing dare warming his eyes.

It was impossible to resist.

Squirming between him and the sofa table, she crossed her arms and stared down at him. "Okay, I'm between you and your computer. This is where you want me, right?"

He frowned. "No. I'd prefer you much closer." He grabbed her hand and yanked her down for a kiss that told her just how much he'd missed her since last evening.

"What do you want to do today?" she asked when they came up for air, and held up a finger to stop the predictable response. "Let me rephrase the question: what *clothed* activity would you like to pursue?"

Matt groaned. "You're no fun."

"I've been reading a travel guide about this area," he told her over breakfast. "There's a small village close by. It's supposed to be 'quaint'. I've always wanted to see a definition of 'quaint'. Want to go there today?"

"Sure. But when did you have time to read a travel guide?"

He sent her a hurt look. "I had all night. All the long eternal lonely night. Alone."

She just smirked at him.

The small village turned out to be busier than they'd expected. Obviously, the tourist industry was thriving. There was even a decent-sized department store, and Jo asked Matt to park close by.

He cursed, but did as she asked. "Come on! Shopping? You want to go *shopping* on your honeymoon?"

"It's not a real honeymoon. And even if it was, why wouldn't I go shopping?"

"This is a practice honeymoon and the same rules apply. You tell me I can't work on my honeymoon, but it's quite okay for you to go shopping? Do you know shopping is the single most horrible torture you can inflict upon a guy? It's right next to Chinese water torture. I'm sure it's in the UN charter that you can't make a guy go shopping on his honeymoon.''

Jo rolled her eyes. ''Fine. You can sit by that pond and feed the ducks while I shop.''

''What do you need so urgently, anyway?'' He glanced down at her sneakers-clad feet. ''Shoes, right? You want to buy some horrible pair of shoes, don't you? Something that'll try to squeeze your feet into permanent triangles, right?''

''Not at all. No shoes. I want to buy you a present,'' she said smoothly. ''Is that romantic enough for a practice honeymoon for you?''

He gave her a distrusting look. ''Are you sure that's what you have in mind?''

''Of course. Trust me.'' She opened the door and got out of the car, and he mirrored her movement on the other side. ''Are you going to bond with the ducks while I'm inside?''

''No way.'' He locked the car and came around to grab her hand. ''I'm going inside too. If I get a present, you get a present.''

They picked a bench by the pond outside the department store to meet at after splitting up for the shopping trip, and it wasn't a surprise for Joanna to exit the store and find Matt already there, reading a newspaper. Most men just didn't know how to shop. It wasn't in their genes. Such a shame. They had no idea what they were missing.

But he did have two large white plastic bags at his feet. Was that her present?

Looked like a *big* present.

''I'm done,'' she said with a satisfied sigh and plopped down next to him, dropping her own bags and trying to sneak a discreet peek into his bags. No go. The contents were boxed and gift-wrapped. "Is that my present?"

Matt closed the newspaper and grinned at her. "I'm impressed. Only two hours, and only three bags?"

"I'm practicing for my honeymoon, remember? Don't want to bore my new husband too much."

"What did you buy?"

"Just…stuff." She poked his bags with her toe, squirming with curiosity. "Did you buy me a present? Is that it?"

"Yup. Did you get me one?"

"I said I would, didn't I?"

"Yes, but I thought that might just be an excuse for you to buy shoes." His eyes danced as she kept trying to sneak glances into the bag. "You like presents, don't you?"

"You know I do. When do I get to open it?"

"Anytime."

"Really? I was sure you'd try to hold off as long as you possibly could."

"Why would I do that?"

She stuck her tongue out at him. "Because that's what you always did."

Matt laughed and stuffed his newspaper in one of his bags. "That's right. It's so much fun to watch you jump up and down with anticipation. But I'll make an exception. Want to open it now?"

The teasing glint in his eyes had her hesitating. He was up to something. "Sure."

Matt pulled the large gift-wrapped box out of one of the bags and dumped it in her lap. She tore the wrapping paper off, then looked at him suspiciously.

''This is a shoebox, isn't it? It looks like a shoebox. You didn't buy me shoes, did you?''

Matt rested his arm on the back of the bench and squinted against the sun, grinning at her. ''Open it and see.''

She removed the lid and browsed through the tissue paper until she found the contents. She pulled them out, for once dubious about his present.

''You bought me Rollerblades?''

Matt winked at her. ''You do know how to ice-skate, after all. Ever tried this?''

''No. Can't say I've ever had a desire to try them, actually.'' He was trying to recreate their first date, she realized, turning the Rollerblades over in her hands. It was sweet. It was also scary.

And not only because she was pretty sure she'd break something if she tried to stand on these wheels.

''There's no ice rink anywhere near here, so this is the closest we can get to the real thing.'' He crouched down in front of her. ''Sit still. I'll get you into them.''

''Shouldn't we wait until we get back to the cottage?''

''Sure, if you want to roller-skate on that potholed country road.''

''No, I suppose that wouldn't be a good idea,'' she muttered. She let him untie the laces on her sneakers, although not at all sure this was what she wanted. ''I don't know, Matt, I kind of like my bones their current shape.''

He was removing her shoes, and sent a hot tingle slithering up her leg when he grabbed her ankle and maneuvered her into one of the Rollerblades. He laced her up, and jiggled the foot in his hand. "How is it? Does it fit?"

She scowled at him. "It fits perfectly. What did you do, sneak into the bedroom last night while I slept and take a cast of my foot?"

Matt grinned, already removing her other shoe. "No. I have a good memory."

The bathtub. The memory zapped to the forefront of her mind, and refused all attempts to be slapped away. They'd taken a bath together, and Matt had made it a challenge for himself to wash her feet without sending her into a paroxysm of ticklish laughter. It hadn't been long until he had mastered that skill, and although his hands moving over her foot had continued to stop her breathing, it wasn't because of ticklishness.

Both her feet were in the Rollerblades, and Matt was sitting on the bench beside her, trying on his own. They looked new as well. "Oh, Lord..." she muttered. "You've never done this before either, have you?"

"It'll be fun. Can't be that different from ice skating, can it?"

"Well, as I remember it, neither of us was particularly good at ice skating."

He winked at her. "All the more reason to cling to each other. That was the best part."

Yes. It had been the best part.

Matt grabbed the other shopping bag and pulled out a helmet. He handed it to her with another wicked smile, then got out a matching one for himself. Then knee pads and elbow pads.

"Matt...this isn't very reassuring."

"If you fall, do you want to be with or without that gear?"

She stared at the orange knee and elbow pads. "It isn't very cool either."

"Trust me on this, love, either way we're not going to look cool."

"Okay. But do we have to look quite so..." She frowned, searching for the perfect word for glow-in-the-dark orange elbow pads. "...*un*cool?"

"Didn't you say something about not wanting to break your bones?"

"Can't you just break my fall?"

"Better safe than sorry. I'm pretty sure we're going to fall, somewhere along the way." He fastened her protective gear quickly, then donned his own.

"Matt...you look absurd."

"Thank you." He kissed her cheek. "So do you." He stood, and, holding on to the bench with one hand, held out a hand. "Come on, Jo. Stand up."

She stood up, hesitantly, and grabbed his hand. "If I fall, will you catch me?"

"Always, Jo. If you'll let me."

She pulled her hand away from his grasp, slowly, holding his gaze. "But you must also allow me to stand on my own wheels."

"Of course."

"And not push me and pull me if I prefer to stumble along myself?"

"How could I? I don't know how to do this either. I'm going to have to cling to you too."

"And if I fall and you don't manage to catch me, you'll pull me to my feet, but still let me dust myself off, won't you?"

Matt laughed, none too steady on his own feet, and

hastily reached out to grab the back of the bench for support. "Jo, you suck at metaphors. Just tell me whatever it is you want to tell me."

Two kids whizzed by, one of them turning around and skating backward as he stared at them. "Look," he called to his companion. "Two old people on Rollerblades!"

"Old people?" Jo stared after them for a moment, then nearly foamed at the mouth as she pushed herself away from the bench. "I'll show him old people..."

A couple of hours later she was feeling rather old as they limped back to the car after resting on their bench for a while. Jo was glad to have her sneakers back on. "I prefer ice skating," she said decisively.

"Me too. Much more romantic."

"No cars on the ice rink."

"This was fun, though."

"Right. I especially liked the part where you went straight through those rosebushes and scared that old lady into throwing her watering can at you."

Matt looked down at his still-damp shirt with a grimace. "Slight miscalculation on my part," he grumbled, starting the car. "I've almost learned how to brake now."

Jo dug her cell phone out of the glove compartment and checked for messages or missed calls. Several—all from the same person. She sighed. Her mother always seemed to think that calling nonstop for fifteen minutes would ensure an answer. She keyed in the number to call her back, remembering that her parents probably still knew nothing about the "marriage". Esther had been unable to reach them, wherever they were.

Helen's voice was bubbling as always, so cheerful it made Jo's teeth hurt. She burst instantly into a monologue on where they were and what they'd been doing, and then switched abruptly to the wedding. "We heard you got married, darling! Congratulations."

"Thank you," Jo said wanly. Helen switched back to an extended travelogue, then called a hasty goodbye as someone spoke to her in the background. Jo tossed the phone on the back seat with a sigh.

"Your parents?" Matt asked.

"My mother. Yeah. Congratulating us."

"That was nice of her."

"Sure. She didn't even ask about you, or if I was happy, she didn't even say she was sorry to have missed the wedding—nothing."

"Did you expect her to?"

"No. Yes." She leaned her head against the window and closed her eyes. "I never expect. That would be pointless. But somewhere there's always hope. You know? Even though I hate myself for it, whenever they call unexpectedly, somewhere at the back of my mind there's always this tiny hope that this time it'll be different."

"But they always let you down."

"Yes." Her eyes opened wide. "Matt, you're analyzing me again, aren't you?"

"Still don't think you have trust issues?"

"No. I don't have 'trust issues.' I have realistic expectations of people."

"Esther has never let you down, has she?"

"Yes. She made me marry you."

Matt laughed, but she ignored him and changed the subject. "And since we're talking about Esther, how do you suppose we do things when we get back? Do we just go straight to her and tell her we're divorcing?''

''Do we want to divorce?''

''We're not married!''

Matt turned the key in the ignition and dragged the seat belt over his middle. ''Let's discuss this back at the cottage, okay?''

He was stalling, wasn't he? Jo didn't blame him. This had now become even more complicated; it looked as though they might be divorcing, but not breaking up. How had everything ended up such a complicated mess?

''So,'' she said, once they had dumped the shopping bags by the door and Matt had got the fire going. She headed straight for the coffee. ''How do we tell her? Suggestions?''

Matt was right behind her, watching her as she made the coffee. ''Well—actually, we don't have to do anything,'' he said. ''She already knows.''

Jo twirled around, nearly throwing a bag of coffee over them both. *''What?''*

Matt shrugged. ''She guessed.''

''And the…sex therapist and the honeymoon…?''

''Attempts to bring us back together. It worked, didn't it?''

''How long has she known?''

Matt took her hand. ''All along, I'm afraid. She planned it all out.''

''So she was never sick?''

''No.''

Jo felt rather indignant when she realized that instead of fury toward the old woman, she was feeling grudging gratitude. Not that she would ever, ever let her know about that.

But if Grandma knew, and Matt knew she knew....

She narrowed her eyes and glared at Matt. "Okay. And why exactly are we here? You let me think my grandmother was dying!"

"No, Jo. I told you all along that I didn't think she wasn't really sick, remember? I didn't know she knew about our break-up until after the therapist. She seemed better then and you were no longer as worried—so..." He looked almost embarrassed. "Okay, so I took advantage. In my defense—it was for a good cause."

Jo scowled. "Nevertheless, deceiving me like this isn't exactly the perfect way to deal with my 'trust issues,' Matt."

"Yes, it is. Can you trust me to have deceived you only because I thought this trip could help us reconcile?"

She held his gaze. "Can *you* trust *me* to make up my mind about reconciliation without manipulating my life?"

Matt winced. "Touché."

"Yeah."

"I'm used to taking charge. Bad habit."

"Well, I can't say I don't appreciate it—sometimes."

"Does that mean I'm forgiven for being a hopeless manipulator?"

Jo closed her eyes and took a slow, deep breath, thinking about her mother's phone call and the superficial way her parents dispensed love from a distance, the way they loved her—but weren't there when she needed them to be.

Matt hadn't been there either when she'd needed him—but she hadn't given him a chance to support her in whatever way he'd thought best, had she? She'd insisted things be done her way.

It hadn't had anything to do with the way he felt about her. But her response had had everything to do with it. She'd let her feelings for Matt cloud her judgment regarding what was logical.

"Yes. You're forgiven."

Matt failed to look relieved. "Are you sure? That was surprisingly easy."

She touched a palm to his shoulder, then curved it around the side of his neck. She pushed at his chest with her hand and walked him backward until he fell into the sofa. "I'm distracted."

Matt grinned at her, and she wasn't sure she was too happy about that. He was supposed to take this a bit more seriously. "Does that lustful look in your eyes mean I don't have to make do with that terrible air mattress tonight?" he asked.

"I don't know," she said. "That depends on how the seduction is."

"Yours or mine?"

"I don't know. Do you want to seduce or be seduced?"

"I get to pick?"

She felt she could suddenly breathe easier as the subconscious decision was suddenly made. "Yes."

"Excellent," he whispered, pushing at her cheek with his nose. "Does that mean I can get you into that tub outside?"

"With or without my demure black swimsuit?"

"With. Absolutely, with. That means I get to peel it off you."

She shivered slightly, and he automatically reached around her, pulling a blanket off the back of the sofa and over her shoulders. "I'm not cold, you idiot," she mumbled against his neck, shrugging the blanket off and unbuttoning the top button of his shirt because he needed a kiss there. "I was trembling with uncontrollable desire. Can't you tell the difference?"

"Sorry. I haven't done the uncontrollable desire thing in over six weeks, you know."

"Do you think you remember how?"

Matt shook his head. "No. I have no idea how this works." He dropped on his back and pulled her over him. "You'll have to show me. Teach me. Guide me. Be gentle with me, will you?"

At any other time, she'd have giggled, but his hand was on her bare waist and she couldn't even breathe. Somehow he'd unbuttoned her shirt while gazing at her with eyes that were deceptively soulful and innocent. She returned the favor. The soft glow from the fire illuminated his skin as she bared it, and the heat of his skin almost seemed to burn her fingers. Too long.

Was he worth the risk?

"Which is more dangerous to me, you or the fire?" she murmured.

"Hmmm?"

She pushed his shirt out of the way and bent her head to kiss his bare shoulder, opened her mouth to gently bite at his flesh, and realized she didn't care.

Some burns were worth it.

CHAPTER TEN

HAPPINESS always made Jo feel as if she could be a poet. So many sensations, everything felt different. Even the air she breathed. She mentioned this to Matt about a microsecond after he woke up, and he rolled his eyes, then rubbed them and yawned. "Of course the air is different. We're up in the mountains instead of in a polluted city."

"It doesn't matter," she told him. "Everything's different when you're happy. The colors, the wind, the sounds you hear—everything."

"You are a dreamer after all," Matt said indulgently, but there was so much warmth in his eyes that she didn't care that he'd all but given her a pat on the head.

"Don't worry, Mr. Romantic, I promise I won't write you a sonnet," she said with a tiny pout, and he laughed.

"I'm glad you're happy, Jo."

"Are you?"

He kissed her temple and pulled her closer. "Yes. I'm happy too. And I'd be even more happy if you'd allow me to sleep for another hour."

"Sleep? You want to *sleep?*"

"Well, you woke me up this early," he complained.

"It's ten o'clock!"

"You kept me up all night, remember?"

Jo pretended to sulk. "The little boy on the Rollerblades was right. You're old."

"It's just been far too long since I've slept with you in my arms. I want more of it."

"Smooth talker."

"Of course, if you keep rubbing yourself against me like that..."

She burrowed even closer. "Yes? Then what?"

"Then I might have to take action."

"We have to go back tonight," she said, sighing. "Our weekend is almost over."

Matt propped his head up on an elbow and automatically reached up in a familiar gesture—but there was no long strand of hair for him to play with. "We have a lot of talking to do, don't we? And we need to plan some rotten trick to pay Esther back. And then there's work. Will you come back and work for us?"

Jo hesitated. "I'm not sure."

Disappointment clouded Matt's eyes, then resignation. "Okay. I understand that you have to think about it. Are you happy in your new job?"

She nodded. "More or less. It's nowhere near as interesting as what I was doing with you—" She slapped his arm. "Stop grinning. I don't mean *that*. I mean the work I did for your company."

"I wasn't thinking anything else."

She ignored that blatant lie. "But my assignments now are probably what I would be doing anyway, if you hadn't taken me on and then given me that promotion. So, I can't complain. I was very lucky Mr. Hastings hired me. Not many companies would have without references."

"You know references weren't a problem."

Anger flashed for a moment, but the fire was

banked, and the agonizing sting that had used to come with the memory wasn't there. It was over—it was not a shadow that would haunt them forever. "I know. At the time I didn't want them."

"We all want you to come back."

"All? Even your father?"

"Especially my father." Matt grinned at her. "You see, he's afraid you'll sue."

She shook her head. "I see. He'll forgive you for consorting with the enemy then. No doubt he'll be pleased with the lengths you've gone to in order to ensure my cooperation in this matter."

"Does that mean you'll come back?"

She paused for a heartbeat. "Yes. I think it does. I'll have to talk with Mr. Hastings, of course, maybe work a few more months while they find a replacement—but I'd like to come back."

There was a light of relief in Matt's eyes, but the tension of his body remained. "There's a catch, of course."

"What?"

"You can't date the boss."

Her heart contracted. "Right."

"But there's nothing to say you can't be married to the boss."

"Matt…?"

He tightened his grasp on her hand, as if he were afraid she would run away. "Marry me again?"

"Just so I can work for you?"

"Yeah. It's my new employment strategy." She started frowning and he touched her face, trying to smooth out the frown. "Bad joke. Of course not. Because I don't want to lose you again."

She stared intently into his eyes. It wasn't *that* important to hear the stupid words, was it? Some people just had trouble saying them. Maybe he was afraid to be the first to say it. Maybe it was just women who obsessed about these things. He wouldn't be asking her to marry him if he didn't love her, would he? But why didn't he *say* it?

Should she say it? Anxiety boiled in her stomach at the thought—and the words stuck in her throat, even though she opened her mouth. No. She didn't dare. Not yet. But that didn't mean that the feelings weren't there—and there was plenty of emotion in Matt's eyes too.

There would be time enough later for silly rituals like saying I love you.

"Well?" Matt was frowning now, a deep look of worry in his eyes. "You're about to say no, aren't you?" He reached for his jeans and pulled a piece of white material from a pocket.

A ribbon?

"It's your hair ribbon from when you were small," Matt explained when he saw her questioning gaze.

"My silk one? I loved that one! I didn't know it still existed. Where did you get it?"

"From your bridal bouquet. It was tied around the stems, remember?"

Jo shook her head. "Grandma made the bouquet. I didn't know. Why did you keep it?"

Matt took her hand again and wrapped it around her ring finger. It was bulky, looking more like a bandage than an engagement ring, but she appreciated the gesture anyway. "Because I'm a sentimental idiot. Don't tell anyone. You're not going to say no, are you?"

How could she say no, now that he'd wrapped one

of her childhood hair ribbons around her ring finger and called himself a sentimental idiot? It was impossible. She loved him. She wanted to marry him—he wanted to marry her. Was she going to let the absence of three small words interfere with their happiness?

She shook her head. "No. I mean, no, I'm not about to say no."

"Watch it, my heart can't take this kind of pressure," Matt joked, but there was strain in his voice. "Well...? What's the verdict?"

She inched from under the sheet. "Wait for me. I'll be right back."

"Where are you going?"

She looked back and grinned at him. "I want to brush my teeth before I say yes."

Matt's victory shout echoed in the mountains through the open window.

The first thing Jo did when she got back to work after the weekend was discuss termination with Mr. Hastings. He cooperated, and Jo could leave her job with just a month's notice.

"Does this have anything to do with your husband?" Mr. Hastings asked, and Jo smiled, feeling for the first time that Matt really was her husband— even though it would probably be a while before they'd make it legal. She curled her hand to better feel the light touch of her fake wedding ring. This time she hadn't removed it before coming to work. Soon she'd have a real one to replace it.

"Yes. We've agreed I'll work in the family firm."

"Wonderful." Mr. Hastings was beaming. "Not that I like losing you, but I'm glad it's to your husband, and not to a competitor." He chuckled. "I was surprised when Matt called to arrange for your day off, but I had my suspicions about the two of you already when I talked to Matt about you coming to work here.''

Jo's world came to a halt. She stared at her boss, then tried to speak, but found her vocal chords uncooperative. "What…"

Mr. Hastings looked surprised, then uncomfortable. "I thought you'd know by now…"

"He asked you to give me a job."

"He supplied references, verbally…"

"I got the job because he asked you to hire me," Jo said tonelessly.

"That's not exactly true. We would have hired you anyway…"

"Would you?"

"Probably… Of course, you didn't have much experience, but with those references…"

Jo rested her head in her hands, feeling tired. "Mr. Hastings, I'd like to withdraw my resignation, if you don't mind."

In a rare display of tactfulness, Mr. Hastings didn't ask any questions. He just whispered quietly, "Of course," and left her alone.

She glanced at her watch. Matt would be picking her up in half an hour. He probably had plans to exchange sly glances and winks with Mr. Hastings behind her back.

She decided to wait in the lobby and spare herself at least that humiliation.

Matt was early, and being deep in thought she didn't even notice his approach before she'd been kissed, pulled out of her chair and was halfway to the car, his arm tight around her shoulders. He was chatting, but she had no idea what he was saying and didn't care. She waited until they were in the car, fastened her seat belt and then turned to him before he could start the car.

"You got me that job."

Matt's face flashed from surprise to annoyance, and then settled in an unreadable expression, but she suspected guilt. "What are you talking about?"

"Don't pretend you don't know what I'm talking about, Matt." She tried to keep her voice level, but she could hear that it trembled with anger. Much as her body did. "Mr. Hastings mentioned he'd suspected something about us when you called him about my job."

Matt shook his head. "It's not that black and white, Jo. You got the job on your own merits. You're more than qualified, more than capable. All I did was…"

"Pull some strings?" *Betrayal,* something was screaming inside, and she could barely see Matt through the red haze of fury. "How could you? You knew I didn't want the job you tried to plant me in. You knew I didn't want anything from you after what happened. You knew I wanted to do things on my own. How could you go behind my back like this?"

"What's the big deal here? You needed a job, Jo, and you wouldn't let me help. It's a tough market and you had only a few months' experience."

"You didn't believe I could get a job on my own."

"I knew it would be difficult. I knew you might be unemployed for weeks or months, and too proud to accept any assistance. I didn't do anything wrong, I did not 'get you the job'—I simply told Carl you'd make a good addition to his team."

"And made him promise not to tell me you'd had anything to do with it."

Matt winced. "I didn't ask him not to tell you. I just mentioned that you wouldn't be too pleased to know we'd talked, that you were very independent."

"Hastings hired me as a favor to you. Not because I'm a good architect, not because of my qualifications, but because you asked him to."

"I wouldn't have recommended you unless I knew you would be an asset to him, Jo. You're being ridiculous."

"You planted me in a job—without telling me."

"No." He leaned toward her, somehow managing to loom over her from the other side of the car. "That's not how it happened. You've got some wires crossed somewhere. I was listed on your résumé as your previous boss, right?"

"Right."

"Carl called me—as anyone would call the former boss of someone he was hiring. I told him the truth about what sort of an employee you were. That's it. I knew it was more than you wanted me to do—that's why I asked him not to mention that we'd talked— but it was not anything more than I'd do for anyone else. I would not call it 'pulling strings'."

Jo sagged in her seat, her heart daring her to believe him, but her mind suspicious. Could it be as innocent as that?

"That's it?"

"I promise you, Jo, that was it. I told him you were a good employee and that I was sorry to lose you, but I did not pull any strings to place you in that position. I respected your wishes. You didn't want my help— so I did only what I would have done for any other good employee—gave you excellent references when asked. Because you deserved it.''

There was something else in his face, and she recognized it because it was an emotion she'd felt often enough herself. Bitterness—because she hadn't trusted him. Again.

He hadn't betrayed her trust. Not this time.

But he had before—and he read the thought on her face.

"Don't go back, Jo," he said, his voice low. "We've been over that."

"I'm furious, Matt!" she said, but her heart wasn't in it anymore.

"I know. You're still hurt. Are you going to let that pride destroy what we have—again? We could have done things better—both of us. I make mistakes. So do you. We're going to be making mistakes our entire lifetime. The only question is whether we want to make them together or separately."

He was talking about spending their lives together, about trust and mistakes and promises—and he still hadn't said he loved her.

Just one little I love you, and she wouldn't have needed that entire speech—but her former certainty that he did love her was wavering now.

"I don't know, Matt—maybe this was just another of our mistakes."

"What the hell are you saying?"

"Remember before?" she asked, struggling to keep her voice even. "You never hugged me in public. Never kissed me if anyone could see us, not even a kiss on the cheek. When you took me ice-skating, you made sure it was on the other side of the city so nobody we knew would see us! I'm not sure you really want to go through with this, Matt. You haven't shown it.''

"You want me to kiss you in public to prove that I love you?''

This wasn't exactly the love declaration she'd been hoping for, especially not in that incredulous, exasperated tone.

"Take me home, please,'' she said, folding her arms and staring straight forward.

Matt leaned back and started the car, shaking his head. "Fine. We'll talk about this later. Where is home? Esther's house or your apartment?''

"Grandma's. It's time to tell her everything's off.''

Matt was silent on the way, then parked the car and accompanied her inside. She didn't comment. Fine. He could explain things to Esther while she tried to figure out how many times she was going to let him break her heart. She said hello to her grandmother, sitting in the living room with her friends, and then excused herself and headed for the stairs. She'd come back down when Matt was gone.

She didn't make it. Halfway there, still in clear sight of the four old ladies, Matt grabbed her, his hands firmly curled around her upper arms. He pulled her toward him, wrapped his arms around her and kissed her until she completely forgot they had an audience.

Their titters reminded her as soon as he let her go again.

"What the hell are you doing, Matt?'' she shrieked as soon as she came to her senses and could breathe again. Barely. He was still holding her so tightly she could feel his heartbeat. It was fast and his body was warm, and she wasn't sure she wanted to be let go.

"Showing a public display of affection," he growled, one of his hands sliding up into her hair to cup her head. He kissed her again, quick and hard, and she knew she didn't want him to release her at all. "In front of Esther and her bridge partners. It doesn't get any more public than that, does it? You wanted a public display of attention, there you are."

"Pretending doesn't count."

"What pretending? Wasn't that a real kiss between a husband and a wife? And aren't we *finally* having a real fight?"

She didn't care anymore who was listening. "Everything's pretend, Matt. Remember? This whole marriage is pretend. You're not my husband. I'm not your wife. Our honeymoon was pretend too, more pretend than I even thought at the time."

"Our honeymoon was the most wonderful weekend of my life, and it'll always be a real one to me. And my 'affections' aren't pretend, Jo. They never were, and they never changed."

Her eyes filled with tears again. From the way she punched his chest with both fists, hard enough to make him wince, and then pulled out of his arms and ran up the stairs, he gathered they weren't happy tears.

So much for professing his love.

He turned to leave, and found four white and gray heads bobbing in a crowd behind him.

"Go after her!" a voice whispered. "Don't blow it! This is your chance!"

"Yes. Now. Don't be so dense, boy. Go."

"We'll be waiting down here with tea and cookies when you two have made up."

"Don't fail us, Matt. We've been terribly disappointed in you so far, but this wasn't too bad."

"That's the trouble with men today. They're so busy being liberated that they forget all about being macho."

Matt turned his head to send them one seething look, and the four ladies turned on their heels and disappeared into the kitchen, though not without sending him a few more well-chosen words of advice.

He ran upstairs to Jo's bedroom door, hesitated a moment, then gingerly turned Jo's doorknob—just checking, he told himself.

It wasn't locked, and that stopped him.

She trusted him not to violate her space.

What the hell. He'd already betrayed her trust. He opened the door, entered and closed it behind him.

Jo was lying face down on her bed, her face buried in a pillow. She glanced up quickly, her eyes red and puffed. "What are you doing in here?" She threw a pillow at him and he caught it. "Go away!"

"No." He crossed the room and sat at her side, tossing down the pillow. "This has gone on long enough."

"Let me guess," she sniffed, grabbing the pillow and burying her face in it again. "We need to talk."

"No. We've talked too much about a subject that's not going to change. We were unlucky and circumstances managed to push us apart. We made mistakes when dealing with those circumstances. We're sorry. We're moving on. It's time to stop wallowing in the past. No more talking."

"Then what are you doing here?"

"I'm going to hold you down and kiss some sense into you, then drag you out tonight and show passionate public displays of affection all over the city whether you like it or not.''

Her shoulders stiffened, then shook slightly in reluctant laughter. ''I see. Did Grandma give you her Bring Back Macho Men speech?''

She was mumbling into her remaining pillow and he sat down on the edge of her bed, grasped her shoulders and turned her over. He touched her tear-stained cheek. ''Maybe. One of them did. They shouted their abuse from afar. What do you think?''

''About what?''

''Macho men.''

''There are pros and cons,'' she muttered. ''Probably like chocolate, wonderful in moderation, painful in large doses.''

Matt's hand shot out to grab her wrist. ''So, if I hold you down and kiss you until you promise to give me a chance...would that be macho in moderation, or too macho?''

''I don't know. Would you stop at a kiss?''

''I suppose that would depend on your response.''

''It might take a lot more than a kiss to make me want to give you a chance.''

''Oh, really? And just what's wrong with my kisses?''

''Nothing.'' Her eyes softened and she was staring at his mouth. ''Absolutely nothing.''

He lowered his head and touched her lips with his, just barely. ''But they're not enough?''

''I believe you,'' she muttered against his mouth. ''That you didn't interfere with my job with Mr. Hastings. Not much, anyway. Not on purpose.''

''Thank you.''

She raised a hand to his cheek, confident now about

his love, but needing to hear it. "I do need something more, Matt."

"What is it?"

"An eloquent speech about those affections you said you had for me."

His lips moved against hers, but there was no sound.

"Matt? I can't read lips."

He grinned—she could read that easily enough. "Maybe it's time you learned. Why do you have to ask? Do you really think I'd let you torture me like this if I didn't love you?"

"Why didn't you ever *tell* me?"

He closed his eyes and grimaced. "You're not going to believe this. You're not going to like it either."

"What?"

"I thought I had told you."

"No, you didn't! You never did!"

"I'm sorry. I meant to. I *thought* it. I said I loved your hair, didn't I?"

"Yes. You said you loved my hair and my eyes and my calves and my—well, quite a few places in between actually, but you never said you loved *me*."

"Isn't it the same thing?"

"No!"

"I love you."

She held her breath for a heartbeat, then nodded regally and looked away. "Well, thanks, that's good to know."

"That's all you're going to say?"

"Yes. You're still in the doghouse for messing with my heart for all this time."

"I see. How long is my sentence?"

"Hmm…. I don't know. Until my hair has grown back, maybe?"

"That's an awfully long time. Will you bring me a bone every now and then?"

She rolled her eyes, but couldn't hide the grin. "Men! You're hopeless."

He leaned closer, and, as a result, she fell backward on the bed. He took quick advantage of that, leaning over her and continuing with his macho man campaign. "But you love us anyway, don't you?"

She took his face between her hands and kissed him fiercely. "Matt…I love *you*."

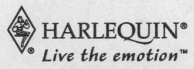

On sale now

girls' night in

21 of today's hottest female authors
1 fabulous short-story collection
And all for a good cause.

Featuring *New York Times* bestselling authors

Jennifer Weiner (author of *Good in Bed*),
Sophie Kinsella (author of *Confessions of a Shopaholic*),
Meg Cabot (author of *The Princess Diaries*)

Net proceeds to benefit War Child, a network of organizations
dedicated to helping children affected by war.

Also featuring bestselling authors...

Carole Matthews, Sarah Mlynowski, Isabel Wolff, Lynda Curnyn,
Chris Manby, Alisa Valdes-Rodriguez, Jill A. Davis, Megan McCafferty,
Emily Barr, Jessica Adams, Lisa Jewell, Lauren Henderson,
Stella Duffy, Jenny Colgan, Anna Maxted, Adele Lang,
Marian Keyes and Louise Bagshawe

RED
DRESS
INK ™

WAR
child

www.RedDressInk.com   www.WarChildusa.org

Available wherever trade paperbacks are sold.

RDIGNIMM

The world's bestselling romance series.

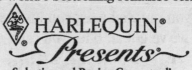

Seduction and Passion Guaranteed!

Legally wed,
Great together in bed,
But he's never said…
"I love you"

They're…

**The series
where marriages
are made in
haste…and love
comes later….**

Don't miss
HIS CONVENIENT MARRIAGE by Sara Craven #2417
on sale September 2004

Coming soon
MISTRESS TO HER HUSBAND by Penny Jordan #2421
on sale October 2004

**Pick up a Harlequin Presents® novel and you will
enter a world of spine-tingling passion and
provocative, tantalizing romance!**

Available wherever Harlequin books are sold.

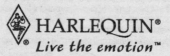

If you enjoyed what you just read,
then we've got an offer you can't resist!

Take 2 bestselling love stories FREE!

Plus get a FREE surprise gift!

Clip this page and mail it to Harlequin Reader Service®

IN U.S.A.
3010 Walden Ave.
P.O. Box 1867
Buffalo, N.Y. 14240-1867

IN CANADA
P.O. Box 609
Fort Erie, Ontario
L2A 5X3

YES! Please send me 2 free Harlequin Romance® novels and my free surprise gift. After receiving them, if I don't wish to receive anymore, I can return the shipping statement marked cancel. If I don't cancel, I will receive 6 brand-new novels every month, before they're available in stores! In the U.S.A., bill me at the bargain price of $3.57 plus 25¢ shipping & handling per book and applicable sales tax, if any*. In Canada, bill me at the bargain price of $4.05 plus 25¢ shipping & handling per book and applicable taxes**. That's the complete price and a savings of 10% off the cover prices—what a great deal! I understand that accepting the 2 free books and gift places me under no obligation ever to buy any books. I can always return a shipment and cancel at any time. Even if I never buy another book from Harlequin, the 2 free books and gift are mine to keep forever.

186 HDN DZ72
386 HDN DZ73

Name	(PLEASE PRINT)	
Address	Apt.#	
City	State/Prov.	Zip/Postal Code

* Terms and prices subject to change without notice. Sales tax applicable in N.Y.
** Canadian residents will be charged applicable provincial taxes and GST.
All orders subject to approval. Offer limited to one per household and not valid to current Harlequin Romance® subscribers.
® are registered trademarks owned and used by the trademark owner and or its licensee.

HROM04   ©2004 Harlequin Enterprises Limited

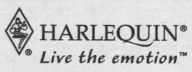

Receive a FREE Hardcover book from

H A R L E Q U I N   R O M A N C E®

in September!

Harlequin Romance celebrates the launch of the series' new cover design by offering you this exclusive offer valid only in September, only in Harlequin Romance.

To receive your
FREE HARDCOVER BOOK
written by bestselling author
Emilie Richards, send us
4 proofs of purchase
from any September 2004
Harlequin Romance books.

All you have to do is send 4 proofs of purchase to:

In the U.S.: Harlequin Books, P.O. Box 9057, Buffalo, NY 14269-9057
In Canada: Harlequin Books, P.O. Box 622, Fort Erie, Ontario L2A 5X3

Name: _____
Address: _____ City: _____
State/Prov.: _____ Zip/Postal Code: _____
Account # (if applicable): _____ 098 KJX DXH4

To receive your FREE HARDCOVER book (retail value is $23.95 U.S./$29.95 CAN.), complete the
above form. Mail it to us with 4 proofs of purchase (found in all September 2004 Harlequin Romance®
books), one of which can be found in the right-hand corner of this page. Requests must be postmarked
no later than October 31, 2004. Please enclose $2.00 (checks made payable to Harlequin Books) for
shipping and handling and allow 4-6 weeks for delivery. New York State residents must add applicable
sales tax on shipping and handling charge, and Canadian residents please add 7% GST. Offer valid in
Canada and the U.S. only, while quantities last. Offer limited to one per household.

Visit us at www.eHarlequin.com and don't forget to be
one of the first to pick up a copy of the new-look
Harlequin Romance books in September!

H A R L E Q U I N
R O M A N C E®
Free Hardcover
PROOF OF PURCHASE

HRPOP09042